. Aotrou & Itroun .

In Britain's land beyond the seas
the wind blows ever through the trees;
in Britain's land beyond the waves
are stony shores and stony caves.

There stands a ruined toft now green,
where lords and ladies once were seen;
where towers were piled above the trees,
and watchmen scanned the sailing seas.

Of old a lord in archéd hall
with standing stones yet grey and tall
there dwelt, till dark his doom befell,
as yet the Briton harpers tell.
No children he had his house to cheer,
his gardens lacked their laughter clear;
though wife he wooed and wed with ring,
who long her love to bed did bring,
his bowers were empty, vain his hoard,
without an heir did to land and sword.
His hungry heart did lonely eld,
his house's end, his banners felled,
his tomb unheeded, long forbode,
till brooding black his mind did goad
a mad and monstrous rede to take,
pondering oft at night awake.

A witch there was, who webs did weave
to snare the heart and wits to reave,
who span dark spells with spider-craft,
and, spinning, soundless shook and laughed;
and draughts she brewed of strength and dread
to bind the live and stir the dead.
In a cave she housed, where winging bats
their harbour sought, and owls and cats
from hunting came with mournful cries
night-stalking near with needle-eyes.
In the homeless hills was that hollow dale,
black was its bowl, its brink was pale;
there silent sat she on seat of stone
at cavern's mouth in the hills alone;
there silent waited. Few there came,
or man, or beast that man doth tame.

'Aotrou & Itroun', first folio of the manuscript.

THE LAY OF
AOTROU AND ITROUN

THE LAY OF
AOTROU AND ITROUN

together with

THE CORRIGAN POEMS

BY

J.R.R. Tolkien

Edited by Verlyn Flieger

With a Note on the Text by
Christopher Tolkien

HOUGHTON MIFFLIN HARCOURT

BOSTON   NEW YORK

2017

First U.S. edition, 2017

For information about permission to reproduce selections from this book,
write to trade.permissions@hmhco.com or to Permissions,
Houghton Mifflin Harcourt Publishing Company, 3 Park Avenue,
19th Floor, New York, New York 10016.

First published by HarperCollins*Publishers* 2016

Library of Congress Cataloging-in-Publication Data is available.
ISBN 978-1-328-83454-6

Printed in the United States of America
DOC 10 9 8 7 6 5 4 3 2 1

CONTENTS

PART THREE:
THE FRAGMENT, MANUSCRIPT DRAFTS AND TYPESCRIPT

PART FOUR:
COMPARATIVE VERSES

PLATES

'The fear of the beautiful fay that ran through the elder ages almost eludes our grasp.'

J.R.R. Tolkien 'On Fairy-stories'

NOTE ON THE TEXT

The Lay of Aotrou and Itroun was once previously printed, in The Welsh Review, Vol. IV, no. 4, December 1945. There are three texts of the poem extant (but no original workings). The first is a good but incomplete manuscript that was apparently overtaken by the second text (very little changed from the first), a fine fair copy on which my father wrote at the end a date: Sept. 23 1930. This is notable, for dates on the fair copy manuscript of The Lay of Leithian run consecutively for a week from September 25, 1930 (against line 3220), while the previous date on the manuscript is November 1929 (against line 3031, apparently referring forwards). Clearly then Aotrou and Itroun interrupted the composition of Canto X of The Lay of Leithian.

The third text is a typescript of the manuscript, incorporating a relatively small number of corrections that had been made to it; this typescript is closely similar to that of The Lay of Leithian, and certainly belongs to this time. Both use the same mode of typing direct speech in italic. Subsequently the typescript was heavily revised, with more than a quarter of the original lines undergoing minor change or complete rewriting: but none of these revisions alter the narrative. My father visited Aberystwyth as an examiner in June 1945 and left with his friend Professor Gwyn Jones several unpublished works, Aotrou and Itroun, The Homecoming of Beorhtnoth, and Sellic Spell. This led to the publication of Aotrou and Itroun in The Welsh Review, of which Gwyn Jones was the editor, at the end of that year, at the editor's request.

There are a few discrepancies between the text printed in The Welsh Review and the typescript which I feel sure was its basis. Nearly all of these are insignificant points of punctuation and spacing. The title in the typescript is Aotrou and Itroun ('Lord and Lady'). A 'Breton Lay.'

It is to be noted that it is incorrect to say that Aotrou and Itroun 'is in alliterative verse, and also incorporates a rhyme-scheme' (Humphrey Carpenter, Biography, p. 168). The poem is in octosyllabic couplets, in style closely related to The Lay of Leithian, and alliteration is decorative, not in any way structural, though here and there it becomes very marked:

> In the homeless hills was her hollow dale,
> black was its bowl, its brink was pale;
> there silent on a seat of stone . . .[1]

But the Lay of Aotrou and Itroun has a longer history, being in fact a development from the second part of a composite poem called The Corrigan (a Breton word meaning 'fairy'), which is also given here. There is no evidence for the date of The Corrigan, though it seems unlikely that any long interval separated it from Aotrou and Itroun.

A pencilled note to the first part of this poem says that it was 'suggested by "Ar Bugel Laec'hiet", a lay of Cornuaille' (in

---

[1] [For a more detailed analysis of the prosody see John Rateliff's discussion in 'Inside Literature: Tolkien's Exploration of Medieval Genres' in *Tolkien in the New Century: Essays in Honor of Tom Shippey*, ed. Houghton, Croft, Martsch, Rateliff and Reid.]

Brittany). The metre of the second part, though distinct from that adopted for Aotrou and Itroun, is not so distinct that lines from it could not be taken up into the second work (and in fact there are more such in the earlier versions of Aotrou and Itroun, rejected in the final revision); but the tale is told in a different manner, and contains no suggestion of the essential element in Aotrou and Itroun that the lord was childless, that he went to a witch to obtain her aid, and that she was the fairy of the fountain.

CHRISTOPHER TOLKIEN

INTRODUCTION

Coming from the darker side of J.R.R. Tolkien's imagination, *The Lay of Aotrou and Itroun*, as well as the two shorter poems that precede and lead up to it, are important additions to the non-Middle-earth portions of his canon and should be set alongside his other retellings of existing myth and legend, *The Legend of Sigurd and Gudrún*, *The Fall of Arthur* and *The Story of Kullervo*. While Tolkien's title makes no reference to the 'beautiful fay' that is the epigraph for this volume – focusing instead on the Lord ('Aotrou') and Lady ('Itroun') who are her victims – the character plays a part in several of Tolkien's poems in his middle years. In addition to the *Lay*, she appears in 'Ides Ælfscýne' (Elf-bright Lady), one of his contributions to the *Songs For The Philologists*, a collection privately printed in 1936. Here an elf-maiden beguiles a mortal man into fairyland; when he returns fifty years later, all his friends are dead. Although Tolkien's poem is in Old English, the character is a commonly recurring one in Celtic folklore, the seductive otherworld female who lures a mortal man.

In the *Lay* she represents a particular subset of this type, a continental Celtic female fairy called a *corrigan*, malevolent, sometimes seductive, whose dangerous attraction embodies both the lure and terror, the 'fear of the beautiful fay' of my epigraph. The *corrigan* figures prominently in all the poems in the present volume, moving from behind the scenes in the first poem, 'The Corrigan' I, based on a Breton ballad, to take centre stage in 'The Corrigan' II, derived from a Breton lay. She becomes an increasingly ominous presence in the two longer versions that Tolkien developed out of 'The Corrigan' II. The sequence charts her increasingly powerful presence as, poem by poem, she takes an ever more active role in the lives of human beings. And finally she foreshadows the greatest and best-known of Tolkien's magical, mysterious ladies of the forest, one also linked to a fountain and a phial: the beautiful and terrible Lady of the Golden Wood, Tolkien's Elven Queen, Galadriel, of *The Lord of the Rings*.

All the poems in this volume are the products of a comparatively short but intense period in Tolkien's life when he was deeply engaged with Celtic languages and mythologies. All the poems derive to a greater or lesser degree from a single source: Theodore Claude Henri Hersart de la Villemarqué's dual-language (Breton and French) folklore collection, *Barzaz-Breiz: Chants Populaire de la Bretagne*, first published in 1839 and reprinted in 1840, 1845, 1846, and 1857. Villemarqué's work was a part of the nineteenth-century folklore movement in Europe and the British Isles, a last-minute effort to capture and preserve the indigenous folk and fairy tales and ballads that were even then rapidly disappearing. What the Grimms' *Kinder- und Hausmärchen* did for Germany, the Child collection of *English and Scottish Popular Ballads* and Percy's *Reliques of Ancient Poetry* did for Britain, and Elias Lönnrot's *Kalevala* did for Finland, Villemarqué intended *Barzaz-Breiz* to do for Brittany (and, it might be added, Tolkien wanted his 'Silmarillion' legendarium to do, imaginatively, for England). This was to recover (or, in Tolkien's case, supply) a folk tradition that would contribute to and validate a cultural identity. Particularly in the cases of the Grimms and Lönnrot the underlying effort was not just to preserve the stories but to discover their lore, and especially their language, the often archaic regional vocabulary or dialect containing the remains of a lost or submerged mythology and worldview, the roots of a native culture.

So it was with Villemarqué. Although Brittany had been a part of France since 1532, it was the Breton identity *celtique* of the *anciens bardes*, as well as the Breton language, that he sought to preserve, and so he was careful to note the regional sources and indigenous dialects for his material, chiefly Léon, Cornouaille, and Tréguier. Immensely popular when it was first published, the *Chants Populaire* was immediately translated into German, Italian, and Polish. An English translation by Tom Taylor was published in 1865 as *Ballads and Songs of Brittany*. Villemarqué was later accused, as were Lönnrot and the Grimms, of tampering with the originals, of 'improving' on the sources. Although the accusations are to some extent true, the underlying myth and folklore elements are authentic, and such accusations have not markedly reduced the popularity of the works in question. *Barzaz-Breiz* has been continuously in print since it first appeared.

Tolkien owned the 1846 two-volume edition, and his signature, John Reuel Tolkien, and the date of purchase, 1922, are written on the flyleaf of each volume. They are listed in a catalogue of his books now held in the English Faculty Library in Oxford, which shows over a hundred entries for Celtic books, histories, grammars, glosses, and dictionaries, as well as primary mythological texts. Many of these, like the Villemarqué, were purchased in the early 1920s. Tolkien was also in this period working on the stories of his own mythology, so it is not surprising that one activity should influence the other, the Celtic content of his studies affecting the form and subject matter of his creative work. Among other efforts, he was at work on *The Lay of Leithian*, a long poem in rhymed octosyllabic couplets that tells the great love story of Beren and Lúthien, a story whose textual history has been edited and published by Christopher Tolkien in *The Lays of Beleriand*.

Christopher's Note on the Text of *Aotrou and Itroun* (see above, p. xi) cites the 'fair copy' on which, as he writes, 'my father wrote at the end a date: Sept. 23, 1930. This is notable,' Christopher continues, 'for dates on the fair copy manuscript of The Lay of Leithian run consecutively for a week from September 25, 1930 (against line 3220), while the previous date on the manuscript is November 1929 (against line 3031, apparently referring forwards).[2] Clearly then Aotrou and Itroun intersected the composition of Canto X of The Lay of Leithian.'

No beginning date for *Aotrou and Itroun* has come to light, but the cluster of dates cited in Christopher's Note – November 1929 against line 3031 of *The Lay of Leithian*, Sept. 23 marking the end of the fair copy of *Aotrou and Itroun,* and Sep. 25 against line 3220 for resumption of work on *The Lay of Leithian* – support his conclusion that in November of 1929 Tolkien interrupted his copying of Canto X of *The Lay of Leithian* for almost a year, and that the product of that interruption was *Aotrou and Itroun*, perhaps even the entire 'Breton' sequence beginning with 'The Corrigan' I.

Because all the poems included here interconnect and

---

[2] Tolkien was in the habit of keeping a log of his progress on the fair copy of *The Lay of Leithian*, noting in the right margin the date by which he had copied so many lines. Thus, 'lines 3076–84 (Canto X), September 1930; line 3220 (Canto X), 25 September; line 3267 (Canto XI), 26 September' (Scull and Hammond *Chronology*, p. 154). No similar log has come to light for *Aotrou and Itroun*.

overlap in their treatment of shared material, it has seemed best for clarity to separate them into shorter sections, each poem followed by notes and commentary. Part I contains the title-poem originally published in *The Welsh Review*. Part II introduces the two (presumably) preliminary poems leading up to it, which Christopher Tolkien has treated together as a composite, since they are conjoined by title. These are 'The Corrigan' I, a story of a changeling, and 'The Corrigan' II, subtitled 'A Breton Lay – after "Aotrou Nann Hag ar Gorrigan" a lay of Leon'. 'The Corrigan' II follows closely the Breton source, but is missing the elements mentioned by Christopher, the couple's childlessness, the Lord's first visit to the witch, and that she is the fairy of the fountain. Part III includes a transcription of the fair manuscript which adds those elements, and facsimile pages from the emended typescript which was the base text for the finished poem published in *The Welsh Review*. Part IV compares Tolkien's poems with verses from the original Breton text and its contemporary French and English translations.

ACKNOWLEDGEMENTS

Thanks go first of all to Chris Smith at HarperCollins and to the Tolkien Trust for initiating this project and inviting me to work on it. I am especially grateful to Chris for his patience and help in overseeing and shaping the volume. My thanks to the Tolkien Trust for granting me permission to reproduce various pages from the author's manuscripts and typescript held in their archive. Particular thanks go to Christopher Tolkien for his contribution and his advice and counsel, and to Baillie Tolkien for her extended help in communication and liaison. All three of them made my work with *The Lay of Aotrou and Itroun* a pleasure. Thank you, one and all.

VERLYN FLIEGER

PART ONE

THE LAY OF AOTROU
AND ITROUN

The Lay of Aotrou and Itroun

as published in *The Welsh Review*

In Britain's land beyond the seas
the wind blows ever through the trees;
in Britain's land beyond the waves
are stony shores and stony caves.

There stands a ruined toft[3] now green   5
where lords and ladies once were seen,
where towers were piled above the trees
and watchmen scanned the sailing seas.
Of old a lord in archéd hall
with standing stones yet grey and tall   10
there dwelt, till dark his doom befell,
as still the Briton harpers tell.

No child he had his house to cheer,
to fill his courts with laughter clear;
though wife he wooed and wed with ring,   15
who love to board and bed did bring,
his pride was empty, vain his hoard,
without an heir to land and sword.

---

[3] homestead

Thus pondering oft at night awake
his darkened mind would visions make   20
of lonely age and death; his tomb
unkept, while strangers in his room
with other names and other shields
were masters of his halls and fields.
Thus counsel cold he took at last;   25
his hope from light to darkness passed.

A witch there was, who webs could weave
to snare the heart and wits to reave,[4]
who span dark spells with spider-craft,
and as she span she softly laughed;   30
a drink she brewed of strength and dread
to bind the quick and stir the dead.
In a cave she housed where winging bats
their harbour sought, and owls and cats
from hunting came with mournful cries,   35
night-stalking near with needle eyes.
In the homeless hills was her hollow dale,
black was its bowl, its brink was pale;
there silent on a seat of stone
before her cave she sat alone.   40
Dark was her door, and few there came,
whether man, or beast that man doth tame.

In Britain's land beyond the waves
are stony hills and stony caves;
the wind blows ever over hills   45
and hollow caves with wailing fills.

---

[4] rob, steal

4

The sun was fallen low and red,
behind the hills the day was dead,
and in the valley formless lay
the misty shadows long and grey.   50
Alone between the dark and light
there rode into the mouth of night
the Briton lord, and creeping fear
about him closed. Dismounting near
he slowly then with lagging feet   55
went halting to the stony seat.
His words came faltering on the wind,
while silent sat the crone and grinned.
Few words he needed; for her eyes
were dark and piercing, filled with lies,   60
yet needle-keen all lies to probe.
He shuddered in his sable robe.
His name she knew, his need, his thought,
the hunger that thither him had brought;
while yet he spoke she laughed aloud,   65
and rose and nodded; head she bowed,
and stooped into her darkening cave,
like ghost returning to the grave.
Thence swift she came. In his hand she laid
a phial[5] of glass so fairly made   70
'twas wonder in that houseless place
to see its cold and gleaming grace;
and therewithin a philter[6] lay
as pale as water thin and grey

---

[5] vial
[6] potion

that spills from stony fountains frore[7]   75
in hollow pools in caverns hoar.[8]

He thanked her, trembling, offering gold
to withered fingers shrunk and old.
The thanks she took not, nor the fee,
but laughing croaked: '*Nay, we shall see!*   80
Let thanks abide till thanks be earned!
Such potions oft, men say, have burned
the heart and brain, or else are nought,
only cold water dearly bought.
Such lies you shall not tell of me;   85
Till it is earned I'll have no fee.
But we shall meet again one day,
and rich reward then you shall pay,
what e'er I ask: it may be gold,
it may be other wealth you hold.'   90

In Britain ways are wild and long,
and woods are dark with danger strong;
and sound of seas is in the leaves,
and wonder walks the forest-eaves.

The way was long, the woods were dark;   95
at last the lord beheld the spark
of living light from window high,
and knew his halls and towers were nigh.
At last he slept in weary sleep
beside his wife, and dreaming deep,   100

[7] frozen
[8] grey

6

he walked with children yet unborn
in gardens fair, until the morn
came slowly through the windows tall,
and shadows moved across the wall.

Then sprang the day with weather fair,   105
for windy rain had washed the air,
and blue and cloudless, clean and high,
above the hills was arched the sky,
and foaming in the northern breeze
beneath the sky there shone the seas.   110
Arising then to greet the sun,
and day with a new thought begun,
that lord in guise of joy him clad,
and masked his mind in manner glad;
his mouth unwonted laughter used   115
and words of mirth. He oft had mused,
walking alone with furrowed brow;
a feast he bade prepare him now.
And '*Itroun mine*,' he said, '*my life,*
'*tis long that thou hast been my wife.*   120
Too swiftly by in love do slip
our gentle years, and as a ship
returns to port, we soon shall find
once more that day of spring we mind,
when we were wed, and bells were rung.   125
But still we love, and still are young:
A merry feast we'll make this year,
and there shall come no sigh nor tear;
and we will feign our love begun
in joy anew, anew to run   130

7

down happy paths – and yet, maybe,
we'll pray that this year we may see
our heart's desire more quick draw nigh
than yet we have seen it, thou and I;
for virtue is in hope and prayer.'   135
So spake he gravely, seeming-fair.

In Britain's land across the seas
the spring is merry in the trees;
the birds in Britain's woodlands pair
when leaves are long and flowers are fair.   140

A merry feast that year they made,
when blossom white on bush was laid;
there minstrels sang and wine was poured,
as it were the marriage of a lord.
A cup of silver wrought he raised   145
and smiling on the lady gazed:
'I drink to thee for health and bliss,
fair love,' he said, *'and with this kiss*
the pledge I pass. Come, drink it deep!
The wine is sweet, the cup is steep!'   150

The wine was red, the cup was grey;
but blended there a potion lay
as pale as water thin and frore
in hollow pools of caverns hoar.
She drank it, laughing with her eyes.   155
'Aotrou, lord and love,' she cries,
'all hail and life both long and sweet,
wherein desire at last to meet!'

8

Now days ran on in great delight
with hope at morn and mirth at night;   160
and in the garden of his dream
the lord would walk, and there would deem
he saw two children, boy and maid,
that fair as flowers danced and played
on lawns of sunlight without hedge   165
save a dark shadow at their edge.

Though spring and summer wear and fade,
though flowers fall and leaves are laid,
and winter winds his trumpet loud,
and snows both fell and forest shroud,   170
though roaring seas upon the shore
go long and white, and neath the door
the wind cries with houseless voice,
in fire and song yet men rejoice,
till as a ship returns to port   175
the spring comes back to field and court.

A song now falls from windows high,
like silver dropping from the sky,
soft in the early eve of spring.

'Why do they play? Why do they sing?'   180

'Light may she lie, our lady fair!
Too long hath been her cradle bare.
Yestreve there came as I passed by
the cry of babes from windows high.
Twin children, I am told there be.   185
Light may they lie and sleep, all three!'

'Would every prayer were answered twice!
The half or nought must oft suffice
for humbler men, who wear their knees
more bare than lords, as oft one sees.'   190

'Not every lord wins such fair grace.
Come wish them speed with kinder face!
Light may she lie, my lady fair;
long live her lord her joy to share!'

A manchild and an infant maid   195
as fair as flowers in bed were laid.
Her joy was come, her pain was passed;
in mirth and ease Itroun at last
in her fair chamber softly lay
singing to her babes lullay.   200
Glad was her lord, as grave he stood
beside her bed of carven wood.
'Now full,' he said, *'is granted me*
both hope and prayer, and what of thee?
Is 't not, fair love, most passing sweet   205
the heart's desire at last to meet?
Yet if thy heart still longing hold,
or lightest wish remain untold,
that will I find and bring to thee,
though I should ride both land and sea!'   210

'Aotrou mine,' she said, *''tis sweet*
at last the heart's desire to meet,
thus after waiting, after prayer,
thus after hope and nigh despair.

I would not have thee run nor ride   215
to-day nor ever from my side;
yet after sickness, after pain,
oft cometh hunger sharp again.'

'*Nay, love, if thirst or hunger strange*
for bird or beast on earth that range,   220
for wine, or water from what well
in any secret fount or dell,
vex thee,' he smiled, '*now swift declare!*
If more than gold or jewel rare,
from greenwood, haply, fallow deer,   225
or fowl that swims the shallow mere
thou cravest, I will bring it thee,
though I should hunt o'er land and lea.
No gold nor silk nor jewel bright
can match my gladness and delight,   230
the boy and maiden lily-fair
that here do lie and thou did'st bear.'

'*Aotrou, lord,*' she said, '*'tis true,*
a longing strong and sharp I knew
in dream for water cool and clear,   235
and venison of the greenwood deer,
for waters crystal-clear and cold
and deer no earthly forests hold;
and still in waking comes unsought
the foolish wish to vex my thought.   240
But I would not have thee run nor ride
to-day nor ever from my side.'

In Brittany beyond the seas
the wind blows ever through the trees;
in Brittany the forest pale   245
marches slow over hill and dale.
There seldom far the horns were wound,
and seldom hunted horse and hound.

The lord his lance of ashwood caught,
the wine was to his stirrup brought;   250
with bow and horn he rode alone,
and iron smote the fire from stone,
as his horse bore him o'er the land
to the green boughs of Broceliande,
to the green dales where listening deer   255
seldom a mortal hunter hear:
there startling now they stare and stand,
as his horn winds in Broceliande.

Beneath the woodland's hanging eaves
a white doe startled under leaves;   260
strangely she glistered in the sun
as she leaped forth and turned to run.
Then reckless after her he spurred;
dim laughter in the woods he heard,
but heeded not, a longing strange   265
for deer that fair and fearless range
vexed him, for venison of the beast
whereon no mortal hunt shall feast,
for waters crystal-clear and cold
that never in holy fountain rolled.   270
He hunted her from the forest eaves
into the twilight under leaves;

the earth was shaken under hoof,
till the boughs were bent into a roof,
and the sun was woven in a snare;   275
and laughter still was on the air.

The sun was falling. In the dell
deep in the forest silence fell.
No sight nor slot[9] of doe he found
but roots of trees upon the ground,   280
and trees like shadows waiting stood
for night to come upon the wood.

The sun was lost, all green was grey.
There twinkled the fountain of the fay,
before a cave on silver sand,   285
under dark boughs in Broceliande.
Soft was the grass and clear the pool;
he laved his face in water cool.
He saw her then, on silver chair
before her cavern, pale her hair,   290
slow was her smile, and white her hand
beckoning in Broceliande.

The moonlight falling clear and cold
her long hair lit; through comb of gold
she drew each lock, and down it fell   295
like the fountain falling in the dell.
He heard her voice, and it was cold
as echo from the world of old,

---

[9] track

13

ere fire was found or iron hewn,
when young was mountain under moon.   300
He heard her voice like water falling
or wind upon a long shore calling,
yet sweet the words: *'We meet again*
here after waiting, after pain!
Aotrou! Lo! thou hast returned —   305
perchance some kindness I have earned?
What hast thou, lord, to give to me
whom thou hast come thus far to see?'

'I know thee not, I know thee not,
nor ever saw thy darkling grot.   310
O Corrigan! 'twas not for thee
I hither came a-hunting free!'

'How darest then, my water wan
to trouble thus, or look me on?
For this at least I claim my fee,   315
if ever thou wouldst wander free.
With love thou shalt me here requite,
for here is long and sweet the night;
in druery[10] *dear thou here shalt deal,*
in bliss more deep than mortals feel.'   320

'I gave no love. My love is wed;
my wife now lieth in child-bed,
and I curse the beast that cheated me
and drew me to this dell to thee.'

---

[10] love-making

14

Her smiling ceased, and slow she said: 325
'Forget thy wife; for thou shalt wed
anew with me, or stand as stone
and wither lifeless and alone,
as stone beside the fountain stand
forgotten in Broceliande.'   330

'I will not stand here turned to stone;
but I will leave thee cold, alone,
and I will ride to mine own home
and the waters blest of Christendome.'

'But three days then and thou shalt die;   335
in three days on thy bier lie!'

'In three days I shall live at ease,
and die but when it God doth please
in eld,[11] or in some time to come
in the brave wars of Christendom.'   340

In Britain's land beyond the waves
are forests dim and secret caves;
in Britain's land the breezes bear
the sound of bells along the air
to mingle with the sound of seas   345
for ever moving in the trees.

---

[11] old age

The wandering way was long and wild;
and hastening home to wife and child
at last the hunter heard the knell
at morning of the sacring-bell;   350
escaped from thicket and from fen
at last he saw the tilth[12] of men;
the hoar and houseless hills he passed,
and weary at his gates him cast.
'Good steward, if thou love me well,   355
bid make my bed! My heart doth swell;
my limbs are numb with heavy sleep,
and drowsy poisons in them creep.
All night, as in a fevered maze,
I have ridden dark and winding ways.'   360
To bed they brought him and to sleep:
in sunless thickets tangled deep
he dreamed, and wandering found no more
the garden green, but on the shore
the seas were moaning in the wind;   365
a face before him leered and grinned:
'Now it is earned, come bring to me
my fee,' a voice said, *'bring my fee!'*
Beside a fountain falling cold
the Corrigan now shrunk and old   370
was sitting singing; in her claw
a comb of bony teeth he saw,
with which she raked her tresses grey,
but in her other hand there lay
a phial of glass with water filled   375
that from the bitter fountain spilled.

---

[12] cultivated land

16

At eve he waked and murmured: *'Ringing*
of bells within my ears, and singing,
a singing is beneath the moon.
Grieve not my wife! Grieve not Itroun!   380
My death is near – but do not tell,
though I am wounded with a spell!
But two days more, and then I die –
and I would have had her sweetly lie
and sweet arise; and live yet long,   385
and see our children hale and strong.'
His words they little understood,
but cursed the fevers of the wood,
and to their lady no word spoke.
Ere second morn was old she woke,   390
and to her women standing near
gave greeting with a merry cheer:
'Good people, lo! the morn is bright!
Say, did my lord return ere night,
and tarries now with hunting worn?'   395

'Nay, lady, he came not with the morn;
but ere men candles set on board,
thou wilt have tidings of thy lord;
or hear his feet to thee returning,
ere candles in the eve are burning.'   400

Ere the third morn was wide she woke,
and eager greeted them, and spoke:

17

'Behold the morn is cold and grey,
and why is my lord so long away?
I do not hear his feet returning   405
neither at evening nor at morning.'

'We do not know, we cannot say,'
they answered and they turned away.

Her gentle babes in swaddling white,
now seven days had seen the light,   410
and she arose and left her bed,
and called her maidens and she said:
'My lord must soon return. Come, bring
my fairest raiment, stone on ring,
and pearl on thread; for him 'twill please   415
to see his wife abroad at ease.'

She looked from window tall and high,
and felt a breeze go coldly by;
she saw it pass from tree to tree;
the clouds were laid from hill to sea.   420
She heard no horn and heard no hoof,
but rain came pattering on the roof;
in Brittany she heard the waves
on sounding shore in hollow caves.

The day wore on till it was old;   425
she heard the bells that slowly tolled.
'Good folk, why do they mourning make?
In tower I hear the slow bells shake,

and Dirige[13] *the white priests sing.*
Whom to the churchyard do they bring?' 430

'A man unhappy here there came
a while agone. His horse was lame;
sickness was on him, and he fell
before our gates, or so they tell.
Here he was harboured, but to-day 435
he died, and passeth now the way
we all must go, to church to lie
on bier before the altar high.'

She looked upon them, dark and deep,
and saw them in the shadows weep. 440
'Then tall, and fair, and brave was he,
or tale of sorrow there must be
concerning him, that still ye keep,
if for a stranger thus ye weep!
What know ye more? Ah, say! ah, say!' 445
They answered not, and turned away.
'Ah me,' she said, *'that I could sleep*
this night, or least that I could weep!'
But all night long she tossed and turned,
and in her limbs a fever burned; 450
and yet when sudden under sun
a fairer morning was begun,
'Good folk, to church I wend,' she said.
'My raiment choose, or robe of red,
or robe of blue, or white and fair, 455
silver and gold – I do not care.'

---

[13] Guide

19

'*Nay, lady,*' said they, '*none of these.*
The custom used, as now one sees,
for women that to churching[14] *go*
is robe of black and walking slow.'   460

In robe of black and walking bent
the lady to her churching went,
in hand a candle small and white,
her face so pale, her hair so bright.
They passed beneath the western door;   465
there dark within on stony floor
a bier was covered with a pall,
and by it yellow candles tall.
The watchful tapers still and bright
upon his blazon cast their light: 470
the arms and banner of her lord;
his pride was ended, vain his hoard.

To bed they brought her, swift to sleep
for ever cold, though there might weep
her women by her dark bedside,   475
or babes in cradle waked and cried.

There was singing slow at dead of night,
and many feet, and taper-light.
At morn there rang the sacring knell;
and far men heard a single bell   480
toll, while the sun lay on the land;
while deep in dim Broceliande
a silver fountain flowed and fell

---

[14] thanks for surviving childbirth

within a darkly woven dell,
and in the homeless hills a dale   485
was filled with laughter cold and pale.

Beside her lord at last she lay
in their long home beneath the clay;
and if their children lived yet long,
or played in garden hale and strong,   490
they saw it not, nor found it sweet
their heart's desire at last to meet.

In Brittany beyond the waves
are sounding shores and hollow caves;
in Brittany beyond the seas   495
the wind blows ever through the trees.

Of lord and lady all is said:
God rest their souls, who now are dead!
Sad is the note and sad the lay,
but mirth we meet not every day.   500
God keep us all in hope and prayer
from evil rede[15] and from despair,
by waters blest of Christendom
to dwell, until at last we come
to joy of Heaven where is queen   505
the maiden Mary pure and clean.

---

[15] counsel

NOTES AND COMMENTARY

Britain's land beyond the seas (l. 1). Brittany, 'Little Britain', Armorica. A western part of France, settled by British refugees from the fifth-century Anglo-Saxon incursion into the western-most parts of the isle of Britain. Tolkien takes care to identify the Breton locale of his poem.

Briton harpers (l. 12). Tolkien is here using Briton interchange-ably with Breton.

witch (l. 27). In spite of the Breton locale and the Breton words that make up the title, Tolkien chooses the English word, derived from Old English *wicce*, with which to introduce his fairy woman. He may have counted on the connotations of 'old, ugly, bent' traditionally associated with the word.

before her cave she sat (l. 40). The cave is a traditional fairy locus. In *The Fairy-Faith in Celtic Countries* Walter Evans-Wentz writes that, 'unlike most water-fairies, the *Fée* lives in a grotto ... according to Villemarqué ... one of those ancient monuments called in Breton *dolmen* or *tí* (dwelling-place) *ar corrigan*' (210).

a phial of glass (l. 70). Usually a tall, narrow vessel, container for a medication or potion.

philter (l. 73). From Latin *philtrum* from Greek *phíltron*, 'love potion'.

frore (l. 75). Archaic past participle of *freeze*, hence *frozen*, *icy cold*.

'Nay, we shall see!' (l. 80). See Christopher Tolkien's comment in his Note. Direct speech set off by italic occurs first in the emended typescript and is replicated in the published version. Since the manuscript versions are in Tolkien's italic hand, there is no opportunity to further distinguish narrative from direct speech.

'Itroun mine' (l. 119). This is the first occurrence in the text of the Breton title 'Lady'. As Tolkien uses it, it seems to be almost a proper name. Throughout the poem, the lord and lady address each other by their Breton titles.

fallow deer (l. 225). Having a reddish yellow coat. From Middle English *falwe*, sallow, Old English *fealo*.

Broceliande (l. 254). This was the great forest of ancient Brittany, where Merlin dwelt with the fay Niniane, and where even now, so goes the legend, he lies imprisoned under a stone. The forest survives today, although greatly reduced in size, as the forest of Paimpont, in central Brittany.

The forest was a standard topos in medieval romance as a landscape contiguous with yet separate from reality, an 'other' world which could on occasion become the actual Otherworld of Celtic myth. Combining real and symbolic associations, the forest became a literary construction with its own rules and associations. Dante made good use of the 'otherness' of the forest, and Shakespeare was not unaware of its function as a setting for unusual or magical happenings.

Tolkien's forests – Mirkwood, Nan Elmoth, Doriath, the Old Forest, Lórien, Fangorn – are some of the most recent in a long and distinguished line of descent. Tolkien used the name *Broceliand*, soon altering the spelling to *Broseliand*, in his *Lay of Leithian*. By September of 1931 it had become, as it subsequently remained in his mythology, *Beleriand*. While the *Broceliande* connection seems clear, we should not overlook an earlier connection of which Tolkien might well have been aware, the notion of *Belerion*, the term used by Diodorus Siculus in the first century BCE for that corner of Britain now known as Cornwall, a Celtic stronghold. The spelling is closer to Tolkien's *Beleriand* than the more attested *Broceliand*.

white doe (l. 260). Not fallow, as in line 225 above. The colour of the doe identifies her as an Otherworld creature. A common motif in medieval ballads and folktales is the hunter who pursues an elusive deer only to have her change into a beautiful woman. Marie de France's *lai* of *Lanval*, which tells of a knight who meets two fairy women by a river, is probably based on the older Breton *lai* of *Graelent*, who follows a white hind through the wood to a place where fairy maidens are bathing in a fountain (see **There twinkled the fountain of the fay** below). The bride of the Irish hero Fionn mac Cumhal appeared to him in the shape of a deer. One function of such an animal is to lead the mortal deep into a wood, traditionally a point of contact with the Otherworld.

There twinkled the fountain of the fay (l. 284). The fountain and the cavern by which the fay stands are traditional points of entry into the Otherworld.

'*O Corrigan!*' (l. 311). This is the first occurrence in the poem of the Breton word which ties *Aotrou and Itroun* to the two earlier poems given in the next section. *Corrigan*, sometimes spelled *Korrigan* or *Gorrigan*, with variants *Corrikêt* or *Corriganed*, is interchangeable in common usage with French *fée*, '*fairy*'. John Rhys's *Celtic Folklore* cites Breton *korr*, 'a dwarf, a fairy, a wee little sorcerer', and *korrigan*, 'a she dwarf, a fairy, a fairy woman, a diminutive sorceress' (Rhys vol. II, 671). The word is glossed in Tom Taylor's *Ballads and Songs of Brittany*, his translation of Villemarqué's *Barzaz-Breiz*, as derived from *kor*, 'dwarf', and *gan*, 'genius', 'spirit'. MacKillop's *Dictionary of Celtic Mythology* defines *corrigan* as a 'Wanton, impish, sprightly female fairy of Breton folklore who desires sexual union with humans', and is often found 'near wells, fountains, dolmens, and menhirs, especially in the forest Broceliand'.

'*With love thou shalt me here requite*' (l. 317). Tolkien here introduces the folklore motif cited in the preceding entry of the fairy woman who tries to seduce a mortal man, as *corrigans* were said to do.

sacring-bell (l. 350). Rung at the Elevation of the Host during the Mass.

Dirige (l. 429). Latin 'guide, direct'. The first word in the Catholic service for the dead. *Dirige, Domine, deus meus, in conspectu tuo viam meam*; 'Guide, O Lord my God, my way in thy sight.' *Dirige* occurs twice in Tolkien's middle period work, once here in *Aotrou and Itroun* and once in *The Homecoming of Beorhtnoth*, where the monks of Ely chant as they bear Beorhtnoth's body from the battlefield. In both cases it follows and counters something pagan, either the triumph of the *corrigan* in the death of the lord, or the victory of the Norsemen at Maldon.

laughter cold and pale (l. 486). The cold laughter of the fay is heard five times throughout the poem, and contrasts with the 'mirth' and laughter of the lord and lady. It thus becomes a leitmotif, a kind of fate-theme both presaging and commenting on the lord's doom, and signalling the hostility of the fairy world toward mortals.

maiden Mary pure and clean (l. 506). Though the poem ends with an invocation to 'the maiden Mary pure and clean' Tolkien nevertheless gives the *corrigan* the last laugh.

PART TWO

THE CORRIGAN POEMS

INTRODUCTION

To trace how Tolkien arrived at the finished *Lay of Aotrou and Itroun* we must go back to what appear to be his first ventures into that territory, the 'Corrigan' poems. Clearly meant as a pair – Christopher Tolkien describes them as a composite – they are a kind of diptych, adjoining works hinged by a shared title, 'The Corrigan'. The general theme in both poems is the same as that of *Aotrou and Itroun*, the interaction of a fairy, a *corrigan*, with the human world. Nevertheless the plots of parts I and II are quite different, and it is only the presence of the *corrigan* that links them.[16]

Where in the long *Lay* Tolkien interchangeably uses the terms *witch*, *fay*, and *corrigan*, here in these shorter poems he uses only the Breton word. *Corrigan*, or *korrigan*, is the feminine diminutive of Breton *corr* or *korr*, 'dwarf', and seems to derive from the notion that these beings have dwindled from their original stature. According to the British folklorist Katherine Briggs, it is because 'they are eager to reinforce their dwindling stock' that 'the Korrigans [the spelling is apparently optional]

---

[16] It is a coincidence worth noting that the word *korigans* appears in the 1891 compendium of folklore known as *The Denham Tracts* (Vol. II, p. 79), where it is in the same word-list as the first known recorded use of the word *hobbits*, another term which Tolkien put to good use in his own work.

make every effort to steal mortal babies and allure mortal men to be their lovers' (Briggs 156). The plot of 'The Corrigan' I turns on the first of these situations, the theft of a mortal baby and its replacement by a changeling, a faerie child. The plot of 'The Corrigan' II, like the published *Aotrou and Itroun*, deals with the second circumstance, the attempt by a faërie woman to seduce or entrap a mortal man, with fatal consequences for the man. The presence of a fountain or well in both poems shows that the *corrigan* was a water-fairy, one who dwelt in or near sites associated with water.

'THE CORRIGAN' I

As noted above by Christopher Tolkien, a pencilled note in Tolkien's hand reading: 'Suggested by "Ar Bugel Laec'hiet" a lay of Cornuoaille', appears in the margin at the head of the fair copy of this poem.[17] This is a reference to entry no. IV in 'Chants Mythologiques', the first section of Villemarqué's *Barzaz-Breiz*. The Breton title, 'Ar bugel Laec'hiet', carries the note 'Ies Kerne' ('of Kerne, or Cornouaille'). Villemarqué's facing-page French translation is titled 'L'Enfant Supposé' and has a corresponding note, 'Dialecte de Cornouaille.' The region cited as Kerne or Cornouaille by Villemarqué and noted by Tolkien is a distinct area on the southwest coast of Brittany, having its own dialect, folk customs, and folklore.

The specific locale notwithstanding, the story itself – the familiar folklore motif of the changeling child and the mother's ruse to unmask him and get her own child back – appears in folk and fairy tales from all parts of Western Europe and the British Isles. In addition to that in Villemarqué there is J. Loth's *Le Nain de Kerhuiton* ('The Fairy of Kerhuiton'), and versions

---

[17] The Breton term *bugel*, is cognate with Welsh *bwg* or *bwgwl*, 'terrifying', as in *bygel* (or *bugail*) *nos*, 'goblin of the night', and appears also in the Breton compound *bugelnoz*, glossed by Mackillop as 'night imp, goblin'.

of the story are to be found as well in Joseph Jacobs' *Celtic Fairy Tales*, and in the brothers Grimm's *Kinder- und Hausmärchen*.

'The Corrigan' I is in rhymed tercets with a shorter rhyming fourth line. All the lines are direct speech. The text below is given as it appears in Tolkien's fair copy, but I have noted in the Commentary section certain revisions from rough draft to final version, which markedly change one aspect of the poem (see below).

The Corrigan

* *
*

I

'Mary on earth, why dost thou weep?'
'My little child I could not keep:
A corrigan stole him in his sleep,
    And I must weep.   4

To a well they went for water clear,
In cradle crooning they left him here,
And I found him not, my baby dear,
    Returning here.   8

In the cradle a strange cry I heard.
Dark was his face like a wrinkled toad;
With hands he clawed, he mouthed and mowed,[18]
    But made no word.   12

---

[18] grimaced

The Corrigan

I

"Mary on earth, why dost thou weep?"
  My little child I could not keep:
A corrigan stole him in his sleep,
    And I must weep.

To a well they went for water clear,
In cradle crooning they left him here,
And I found him not, my baby dear,
    Returning here.
In the cradle a strange cry I heard.
Dark was his face like a wrinkled toad;
With hands he clawed, he mouthed and mowed,
    But made no word.

And ever he cries and claws the breast:
Seven long years, and still no rest;
Unweaned he wails, though I have pressed
    My weary breast.

O Mary Maiden, who on throne of snow
Thine own babe in thine arms dost know,
Joy is round thee; but I have woe
    And weep below.

And ever he cries and claws the breast:
Seven long years, and still no rest;
Unweaned he wails, though I have pressed
    My weary breast.   16

O Mary Maiden, who on throne of snow
Thine own babe in thine arms dost know,
Joy is round thee; but I have woe
    And weep below.   20

Thy holy child thou hast on knee,
But mine is lost. A! where is he?
Mother of pity, pity me
    Who cry to thee!'   24

'Mary on earth, do not mourn!
Thy child is not lost. He will return.
Go to the hermit that dwells by the burn,
    And counsel learn.'   28

'Why dost thou knock? Why dost thou weep?
Why hast thou climbed my path so steep?'
'My little child I could not keep,
    And ever I weep.'   32

'Bid them grind an acorn, bid them feign
In a shell to cook it for master and men
At midday hour. If he sees that then,
    He will speak again.   36

And if he speaks, there hangs on thy wall
A cross-hilt sword old and tall –
Raise it to strike and he will call,
    And the spell will fall.'   40

'What do they here, mother of me?
I marvel much at what I see
In this kitchen to-day. What can it be?
    That I here see?'   44

'What wouldst thou son? – on embers hot
Meal for men in a white pot
They grind and cook, that our food be got.
    Why should they not?'   48

'Mast[19] in a shell for many men!
I saw the first egg before the white hen,
And the acorn before the oak in den[20] –
    There were strange things then.   52

The land of Brezail was fair, I trow:
I saw once silver birds enow,
And acorns of gold on every bough.
    This is stranger now!'   56

'Thou hast seen too much, too much, my son!
Thy words are wild, thy looks are wan.
This sword shall make thy dark blood run,
    Thou art not my son!'   60

---

[19] fallen nuts
[20] glen, dell

'A! stay, a! stay thy cruel hand!
Soft thy son lay in our land,
But thou wouldst slay one who did stand
    A prince in our land.'   64

'Mary on earth, what didst thou find
When thou didst look in the room behind?
In cloth of silver who did wind
    The child of thine?'   68

'I looked on my child with heaven's bliss,
I stooped to the cradle him to kiss,
And he opened the sweet eyes of his
    For me to kiss.   72

He sat him up and arms he spread,
He caught my breast and to me said:
"A! mother of me, I am late in bed!
    My dream is sped."'   76

* *
*

NOTES AND COMMENTARY

Although there are similar tales about changeling children in other Celtic mythologies, they are cast in prose. I have not found any versions in verse form other than in Villemarqué.

Mary on earth (l. 1). With these three words of address the voice that opens the poem establishes the situation, the heavenly Mary's concern for the earthly mother, and sets up the conflict between pagan folklore and Christianity.

a corrigan stole him in his sleep (l. 3). Thomas Keightley's discussion in the 'Brittany' section of his 1892 *The Fairy Mythology* cites Villemarqué, and gives a synopsis of,

> 'the story of a changeling. In order to recover her own child the mother is advised, by the Virgin, to whom she has prayed, to prepare a meal for ten farm-servants in an egg-shell, which will make the Korrid [*sic*] speak, and she is then to whip him well till he cries, and when he does so he will be taken away' (Keightley, 436).

A variant in which the mother, not the child, is abducted into Faërie is given in an early Scottish account of the Faërie Otherworld, *The Secret Commonwealth of Elves, Fauns and*

Fairies. The author, the Reverend Robert Kirk, Minister of Aberfoyle, Scotland, wrote in 1691 that,

> 'Women are yet alive who tell they were taken away when in Child-bed to nurse Fairie Children, a lingering voracious Image of them being left in their place, (like their Reflexion in a Mirrour)' (Kirk 72).

To a well they went for water clear (l. 5). The poem does not specify who 'they' are, but in the original Breton and the French translation it is not some anonymous group but rather the mother who left her baby. Villemarqué's French translation has the mother say *En allant à la fontaine puiser de l'eau, je laissai mon Laoik dans son berceau*, 'Going to the well to draw water, I left my Laoik [a proper name] in his cradle'.

like a wrinkled toad (l. 10). The appearance of the faerie child is a convention. In contradiction to one of the traditional fairy epithets, 'Fair Folk', changeling babies are traditionally described as ugly, wizened, preternaturally small, and slow of growth.

O Mary Maiden (l. 17). The prayer derives from the belief, described by Katherine Briggs, that Corrigans 'have . . . a great hatred of all Christian symbols and in particular of the Virgin Mary, who takes under her special protection those human infants whom the Korrigans attempt to steal' (156).

a cross-hilt sword (l. 38). The cross-hilt makes the sword a Christian symbol, and therefore abhorrent to the *corrigan* (see **O Mary Maiden** above and discussion of revisions below). It is also, of course, made of iron, a substance inimical to fairies, and often used to drive them away.

the first egg (l. 50), which reveals the changeling baby's age, is a standard trope in fairy lore. Loth's *Le Nain de Kerhuiton*, a collection of Breton folklore, records a similar episode.

> Upon seeing water boiling in a number of egg-shells ranged before an open fire a *polpegan*-changeling is so greatly astonished that he unwittingly speaks for the first time, and says 'Here I am almost one hundred years old, and never such a thing have I yet seen!'
>
> (Loth, *Le Nain de Kerhuiton*, quoted in Evans-Wentz 212)

land of Brezail (l. 53). Brezail, or Hy-Breasail, was a name for one of the Celtic Otherworlds, and figures in Celtic myth as a magic land in the west. It appears in Villemarqué's Breton as 'Brezal' and in his French paraphrase as 'Brézal'. Tolkien's comment in 'On Fairy-stories' that Hy-Breasail has dwindled from its mythic estate to become the 'mere Brazils, the land of red-dye-wood' (*MC* 111), suggests his disaffection for the rationalization of myth into history.

silver birds, acorns of gold (ll. 54–55). These recall the white birds and magical fruits and berries seen by the mariners of the Celtic *imramma* ('Voyagings') such as the *Navigatio* of St. Brendan and the very similar *Voyages* of Bran and Mael Duin. Tolkien's own *Imram*, appended to *The Notion Club Papers* (*Sauron Defeated* pp. 296–9) and based on the *Navigatio*, mentions a tree with what appear to be white leaves which suddenly 'as white birds rose in wheeling flight' (*SD* 298).

our land (ll. 62 & 64). This mention by the changeling child is a reference to the Celtic Otherworld, which has its own royal hierarchy, and is generally envisioned as contiguous with but invisible to this world. The Otherworld is often located over the sea or under a lake, but caves, grottoes, and forests can also be entrances to the fairy world, and humans can cross the boundary without knowing it.

the room behind (l. 66). In the cases of changeling children, *corrigans* can clearly enter and leave the 'real' world at will.

cloth of silver (l. 67). The human child, still wrapped as faërie royalty, has been surreptitiously returned by the *corrigan* when the spell falls.

For the most part the revisions from rough drafts to fair copy are minor – the alteration of a word or phrase here or there, for example from the 'Mari goant' and 'Mary la belle' of the Breton and French source to Tolkien's 'Mary on earth'. However, one change – or sequence of changes – between early draft and final copy involves a radical departure from the Breton source. Both the change and the nature of the change are worth noting. In the final copy lines 37–40 read as follows:

> And if he speaks, there hangs on thy wall
> A cross-hilt sword old and tall –
> Raise it to strike and he will call,
> And the spell will fall.

The earlier draft is quite different:

> And if he speak, then beat him well,
> Beat him sore till he doth wail.
> They will come at his call, as at a spell;
> They will not fail!

These last lines are a fair translation of the Breton, which I quote here to give a sense of the shape and flavor of the original language, that language which led Tolkien to the discovery of the particular culture whose myth and folklore are embedded in it.

> Pa'n deuz prezeget flemm-han, flemm!
> Pa eo bet flemmet ken, a glemm;
> pa eo klevet, he lammer lemm.
>
> (*Barzaz-Breiz* 52)

Here is the passage in Villemarqué's prose French translation:

> Quand il a parlé, fouettez-le, fouettez-le bien; quant il a été bien fouetté, il crie; quand il a été entendu, il est enlevé promptement.
>
> (ibid. 53)

The motif of the beating is apparently a more standard way of exorcising the changeling than the cross-hilt sword. Loth reports just such an end to the egg-shell episode described above. When the changeling child speaks and reveals his age, the mother responds by beating him.

> 'Ah! son of Satan!' then cries the mother, as she comes from her place of hiding and beats the *polpegan* – who thus by means of the egg-shell test has been tricked into revealing his demon nature.
>
> (Loth, *Le Nain de Kerhuiton* quoted in Evans-Wentz 212)

Tolkien's decision to substitute the threat of the cross-hilt sword for the savage beating of the changeling child explicitly matches Christianity against pagan faërie, and harmonizes more nearly with the dialogue between the earthly Mary and the heavenly Mary which is the poem's occasion. A similar shift occurs in lines 57–60, which in Tolkien's fair copy are as follows:

> Thou hast seen too much, too much, my son!
> Thy words are wild, thy looks are wan.
> This sword shall make thy dark blood run,
>   Thou art not my son!

where his earlier draft has:

> Thou hast seen too much, too much, my son!
> Thy words are wild, thy looks are wan.
> I will beat thee, beat thee till the blood run.
>   A, cry, my son!

Again, the earlier version is a fair approximation of the Breton poem, though Tolkien has substituted description for the onomatopoeic sound effects of the original.

> – Re draou a welaz-te, va map;
> *Da flap! da flip! da flip! da flap!*
> *Da flip*, potr koz! ha me da grap!
>   (*Barzaz-Breiz* 52)

which are replicated in Villemarqué's translation:

Tu as vu trop de choses mon fils: *clic! clac! clic! clac!* Petit viellard, ah!, je te tiens!

>   (ibid. 53)

In the same vein, lines 61–64, which in Tolkien's fair copy read:

> A! stay, a! stay thy cruel hand!
> Soft thy son lay in our land,
> But thou wouldst slay one who did stand
>   A prince in our land.

were in the earlier version,

Ah stay, ah stay thy cruel hand;
For soft thy son lay in our land,
But thou dost beat one who did stand
    Once King in our land!

Here both Tolkien's fair copy and his draft version depart markedly from the Breton source. While the fair copy eliminates the last trace of physical violence, a change dictated by the alterations in the previous stanzas, both fair copy and rough draft agree in having it be the changeling child who is faërie royalty (either prince or king), whereas in both the Breton original and Villemarqué's French rendering it was the human child who was king in the faërie land ('I did not harm your son; he is our king in our land').

– Sko ket gant-han, lez-han gan-i;
Na rann-me droug da da hini,
'Ma brenn er bro-ni gan-e-omp-ni.—

(ibid. 52)

– Ne le frappe pas, rends-le-moi; je ne fais aucun mal au tien; il
est notre roi dans notre pays. –

(ibid. 53)

'THE CORRIGAN' II

A Breton Lay – after: 'Aotrou Nann Hag ar Gorrigan'
a lay of Leon

Tolkien's subtitle here is a more formal citation of source than his pencilled jotting in the margin of 'The Corrigan' I. 'Aotrou Nann Hag ar Gorrigan' ('Lord Nann and the Corrigan') is entry number III in Hersart de la Villemarqué's collection. Like 'Ar Bugel Laec'hiet' it is printed both in Breton with the note 'Es Leon' ('of Leon'), and also in French, with the French title 'Le Seigneur Nann et la Fée' and the note 'Dialecte de Léon'. Like Cornouaille, the Léon of the subtitle is a distinct region of Brittany, the extreme western horn, and is to the folklorist an area clearly separate from Cornouaille in dialect, custom, and dress. Nevertheless, there are obvious pan-regional correspondences, as evidenced by the recurrence of the word *corrigan*.

Like 'Ar Bugel Laec'hiet' this poem closely follows a Breton source, in which a lord, newly the father of twins, promises to bring his wife a 'fallow deer' to celebrate the birth of their son. He pursues a white doe who leads him to the fountain of the fay. Attempting to seduce him, she threatens him with death if he will not 'wed' her. He refuses and, as she has predicted, dies 'on the third morning'. His wife dies of grief, and they are buried together. The story lacks the 'counsel cold' that in Tolkien's later and longer *Aotrou and Itroun* darkens the mind of the childless lord and makes him deliberately seek out the fay in order to procure a magical potion to aid fertility. Without this complication, the plot of 'The Corrigan' II follows the standard fairy tale formula of an innocent mortal's accidental incursion into the faërie world and its consequences, a plot that, in his essay 'On Fairy-stories', Tolkien called 'Faërian Drama' and described as 'those plays which according to abundant records the elves have often presented to men' (*MC* 142).

The Breton ballad has a number of analogues in other cultures. The Child collection offers three English versions in which the fairy is a mermaid,[21] while Villemarqué cites a Danish *Sire Olaf dans la danse des Elves* (Villemarqué vol. 1, p. 46). For a fuller discussion of the other versions see Jessica Yates' 'The Source of "The Lay of Aotrou and Itroun"' in *Leaves From the Tree: J. R. R. Tolkien's Shorter Fiction,* a collection of papers presented at the Fourth Tolkien Society Workshop, and published by the British Tolkien Society, London, 1991.

Like 'The Corrigan' I, 'The Corrigan' II is a ballad, but with different subject matter, greater length, and a more complex rhyme scheme – three lines rhyming a a a, and the b-line, the refrain, ending in an unstressed syllable and rhyming with the b-line in the next verse. Preceding the fair copy are two shorter drafts, which are essentially rough workings with many crossings-out and marginal emendations.

---

[21] Tolkien also wrote a mermaid poem in Old English, 'Ofer Wídne Gársecg' (Across the Broad Ocean), included in *Songs For The Philologists*, pp. 14–15.

The Corrigan

A Breton Lay – after: 'Aotrou Nann Hag ar Gorrigan'
a lay of Leon

II

See how high in their joy they ride,
The young earl and his young bride!
May nought ever their joy divide,
    Though the world be full of wonder.   4

There is a song from windows high.
Why do they sing? Light may she lie!
Yestreve there came two babes' cry
    As I stood thereunder.   8

A manchild and a fair maid
Were as lilies fair in cradle laid,
And the earl to his young wife said:
    'For what doth thy heart hunger?   12

A son thou hast given me,
And that will I find for thee,
Though I should ride o'er land and lea,
    And suffer thirst and hunger.   16

The Corrigan

. A Breton Lay — after : "Aotrou Nann Hag ar Gorrigan"
a lay of Leon.

II

See how high in their joy they ride,
The young earl and his young bride!
May nought ever their joy divide,
    Though the world be full of wonder.

There is a song from wind ows high.
Why do they sing? Light may she lie!
Yestreve there came two babes' cry
    As I stood thereunder.

A manchild and a fair maid
Were as lilies fair in cradle laid,
And the earl to his young wife said :
    "For what doth thy heart hunger?"

A son thou hast given me,
And that will I find for thee,
Though I should ride o'er land and lea,
    And suffer thirst and hunger.

For fowl that swims the shallow mere?
From greenwood the fallow deer?"
"I would fain have the fallow deer,
    But I would not have thee wander."

His lance of ash he caught in hand,
His black horse bore him o'er the land.
Under green boughs of Broceliand
    His horn winds faintly yonder.

A white doe startled beneath the leaves,
He hunted her from the forest-caves ;
Into twilight under the leaves
    He rode on ever after.

The earth shook beneath the hoof ;
The boughs were bent into a roof,
And the sun was woven in that woof,
    And afar there was a laughter.

5

For fowl that swims the shallow mere?
From greenwood the fallow deer?'
'I would fain have the fallow deer,
    But I would not have thee wander.'   20

His lance of ash he caught in hand,
His black horse bore him o'er the land.
Under green boughs of Broceliand
    His horn winds faintly yonder.   24

A white doe startled beneath the leaves,
He hunted her from the forest-eaves;
Into twilight under the leaves
    He rode on ever after.   28

The earth shook beneath the hoof;
The boughs were bent into a roof,
And the sun was woven in that woof,
    And afar there was a laughter.   32

The sun was fallen, evening grey.
There twinkled the fountain of the fay
Before the cavern where she lay,
    A corrigan of Brittany.   36

Green was the grass, clear the pool;
He laved his face in water cool,
And then he saw her on silver stool
    Singing a secret litany.   40

The moon through leaves clear and cold
Her long hair lit; through comb of gold
Each tress she drew, and down it rolled
    Beside her falling fountain.   44

He heard her voice and it was cold;
Her words were of the world of old,
When walked no men upon the mould,
    And young was moon and mountain.   48

'How darest thou my water wan
To trouble thus, or look me on?
Now shalt thou wed me, or grey and wan
    Ever stand as stone and wither!'   52

'I will not wed thee! I am wed;
My young wife lieth in childbed,
And I curse the beast that long me led
    To thy dark cavern hither.   56

I will not stand here turned to stone,
But I will leave thee cold alone,
And I will ride to mine own home
    And the white waters of Christendom.'   60

'In three days then thou shalt die,
In three days on thy bier lie!'
'In three days I shall live at ease,
And die but when God doth please
    In the brave wars of Christendom.   64

But rather would I die this hour
Than lie with thee in thy cold bower,
O! Corrigan, though strange thy power
    In the old moon singing.'   68

            * *
             *

'A! mother mine, if thou love me well,
Make me my bed! My heart doth swell,
And in my limbs is poison fell,
    And in my ears a singing.   72

Grieve her not yet, do not tell!
Sweet may she keep our children well;
But a corrigan hath cast on me a spell,
    And I die on the third morning.'   76

On the third day my lady spake:
'Good mother, what is the noise they make?
In the towers slow bells shake,
    And there is sound of mourning.   80

Why are the white priests chanting low?'
'An unhappy man to the grave doth go.
He lodged here at night, and at cock-crow
    He died at grey of morning.'   84

'Good mother, say, where is my lord?'
'My child, he hath fared abroad.
Ere the candles are set upon the board,
    Thou wilt hear his feet returning.'   88

'Good mother, shall I wear robe of blue
Or robe of red?' 'Nay, 'tis custom new
To walk to church in sable hue
    And black weeds wearing.'   92

I saw them pass the churchyard gate.
'Who of our kin hath died of late?
Good mother, why is the earth so red?'
'A dear one is buried. We mourn him dead
    Our black weeds wearing.'   98

They laid her beside him in the night.
I heard bells ring. There was taper light.
    Priests were chanting a litany.
Darkness lay upon the land,   102
But afar, in pale Broceliand
    There sang a fay in Brittany.

NOTES AND COMMENTARY

from the forest eaves; Into twilight under the leaves (ll. 26 & 27). The lord's progression shows him riding unaware through an entry-portal into the Otherworld. Celtic Otherworlds are various in their natures and appearances, but one of the most evocative is the deep forest, far from the human community, whose shadowed reaches are the habitat of all kinds of 'otherness', from strange birds and beasts to wild men to creatures of the other reality of faërie.

There twinkled the fountain of the fay (l. 34). Note that this was retained unchanged in the final poem, *Aotrou and Itroun*. In this earlier version the *corrigan* is more clearly pictured as a water-fairy. The fountain where the *Fée* was seated seems to be one of those sacred fountains, which, as Villemarqué says, are often found near a *'grotte aux Fées'*, called a *'Fontaine de la Fée'*, or in Breton, *'Feunteun ar corrigan'* (Villemarqué vol. 1, p. 46).

A corrigan of Brittany (l. 36). Unlike the dwarfish child-stealer of 'The Corrigan' I, the *corrigan* of this poem represents a figure more typical of myth than of folklore (though she appears in both), the human-size fairy who can appear as either a beautiful woman or an old hag. As used here the word *corrigan* seems more nearly akin in meaning to 'fairy' than to 'spirit' or 'goblin', as in 'The Corrigan' I, for both Villemarqué and Tolkien use the words *fée* (or *fay*) and *corrigan* interchangeably.

She is seen here as she is most often pictured in fairy-lore, near water, seductively combing out her long hair. Tolkien himself later applied the term *fay* to his Guinever in *The Fall of Arthur*, written circa 1934 but not published until 2013, where she is described as being 'fair as fay-woman in the world walking for the woe of men'.

Now shalt thou wed me (l. 51). See note to *Aotrou and Itroun* above on '*With love thou shalt me here requite*' (p. 25).

Make me my bed! (l. 70). A traditional ballad line signifying the Lord's awareness of his fatal illness. It occurs with incremental repetition in the Child ballad 'Lord Randall', where the dying Lord, who comes home from 'the greenwood' where he has been poisoned by his lover, first tells his mother:

'Mother mak my bed soon, For I'm wearied wi huntin, and fain wad lie down.'

Halfway through, the line changes to:

'Mother mak my bed soon, For I'm sick at the heart, and I fain wad lie down.'

Tolkien's use of the trope may be a conscious reference to the 'Lord Randall' ballad.

Good mother, what is the noise they make? (l. 78). In Villemarqué's 'Notes et Éclaircissements' on the ballad he includes six stanzas in French which, he writes, 'le peuple la chante encore dans la haute Bretagne', and which are 'une traduction exacte de stances bretonnes'.

> – Oh! dites-moi, ma mère, ma mie,
> Pourquoi les sings (cloches) sonnent ainsi?

> – Ma fille, on fait la procession
> Tout à l'entour de la maison.

> – Oh! Dites-moi, ma mère, ma mie,
> Quel habit mettrai-je aujourd'hui?

> – Prenez du noir, prenez du blanc;
> Mais le noir est plus convenant.

> *   *   *   *   *

> – Oh! dites-moi, ma mère, ma mie,
> Pourquoi la terre est refrâichie?

> – Je ne peux plus vous le cacher:
> Votre mari est enterré.

> (ibid. 46)

There sang a fay (l. 104). Contrast with the laughter of the fay in the published *Aotrou and Itroun*. Tolkien's poem, darker than its *Barzaz-Breiz* source, closes with the singing of the fay. He has chosen to omit the Breton ending in which the wife is buried in the same grave as her lord, and twin holly-oaks (pagan emblems of rebirth) grow from the tomb. In their branches are two white doves who sing at sunrise and fly up toward heaven.

PART THREE

THE FRAGMENT, MANUSCRIPT DRAFTS AND TYPESCRIPT

THE FRAGMENT

This incomplete, untitled poem, breaking off in mid-sentence, marks Tolkien's transition, first from the two ballad-like 'Corrigan' poems to the much longer and more psychologically complex *Aotrou and Itroun*, and second from reworking existing material to producing a newly created poem. The fragment, a brief 29 lines, is written in italic script on a ragged sheet of lined paper whose dog-eared condition distinguishes it from the relatively good state of the 'Corrigan' pages.

The fragment has no title, though it obviously presages Tolkien's much longer and more elaborate treatments of both the fair-copy manuscript and the typescript of 'Aotrou and Itroun', as well as the final version published in *The Welsh Review*. The verse is alliterative and unrhymed, though the line is metrical, in iambic tetrameter. The story breaks off at the moment of the lord's approach 'with lagging feet' to the cave of the fay.

The fragment is significant for its first introduction into the story of the childlessness of the lord and his initial visit to the fay, neither of which element is present in its precursors.

Of old a lord in archéd halls,
whose standing stones were shaggy and grey,
whose towers were tall o'er trees upraised,
once dwelt till dark his doom befall.
No child he had to cheer his house,
no son as heir to sword and land,
though wife he ~~had~~ wooed and wedding,
and long his bed in love she shared.
Long did his heart a ~~troubl~~ eld,
his house's end, an unheeded tomb,
forebode, and blackly brooding burned
his mind to a mad and monstrous rede.
~~A witch there~~ ~~was~~ marvels contrived
and spun dark spells with spider-craft;
and potions brewed of power and dread.
In a cave she housed where rats and owls
were harbour'd straight from hunting came,
night-stalking near with needle-eyes.
In the houseless hills in a hollow dale
black was ~~the~~ bred and bleak its edge
rimmed with maian rocks and cold.
There sat she silent on ~~her~~ seat of stone
at cavern's mouth in cries and spake
to her secret self. There seldom ~~came~~ led
or man at least that man hath known.
Yet there one day as drooping low
a sullen sun in sinking dead,
and red his rocks ~~the~~ rays did slant,
there low alone with lagging feet

𝔔'

𝔔

④

Of old a lord in archéd halls,
whose standing stones were strong and grey,
whose towers were tall o'er trees upraised,
once dwelt till dark his doom befell.
No child he had to cheer his house,
no son or heir to sword and land,
though wife he wooed and wed with ring,
and long his bed in love she shared.
Long did his heart a lonely eld,
his house's end, an unheeded tomb
forebode, and blackly brooding bound
his mind to a mad and monstrous rede.[22]
A witch there was who webs contrived
and span dark spells with spider-craft
and potions brewed of power and dread.
In a cave she housed where cats and owls
their harbour sought from hunting came,
night-stalking near with needle-eyes.
In the houseless hills was a hollow dale
black was its bowl and bleak its edge
returned[23] with ruinous[24] rocks and cold.
There sat she silent on seat of stone
at cavern's mouth or cried and spake
to her secret self. There seldom dared
or[25] man or beast that man hath tamed.
Yet there one day as drooping low
a sullen sun was sinking dead,
and red the rocks the rays did slant,
that lord alone with lagging feet

---

[22] decision
[23] bent; back
[24] fallen
[25] 'or' in the sense of 'either'

THE MANUSCRIPT DRAFTS

A fair copy, described in Christopher Tolkien's Note on the Text as, 'a good but incomplete manuscript' of five pages clipped together as a unit, incorporates the fragment, cast now in rhymed couplets instead of alliterative verse, and preceded by an introductory verse locating the scene 'in Britain's land beyond the seas', that is to say, in Brittany. It covers the Lord's first visit to the fay, and the birth of two children, and goes as far as the Lord's adjuration to Itroun to name her desire, but is missing a page. The first three pages, consisting of respectively 42, 44, and 42 lines numbered in the margin up to line 128, are contiguous and end on the third complete page with the lord's speech to his wife. I give the line number as it appears in the manuscript.

> A merry feast we'll make this year,
> and there shall sit nor sigh nor tear;
> and we will feign our love begun   125
> in joy anew, anew to run
> down happy paths – and yet maybe,
> we'll pray that this time we may see

The fourth page, written in a slightly smaller hand, as though part of a different copy, and comprising only 32 lines, is not continuous with the preceding three, but appears to be an inclusion from a different text. It opens with line 221 (again, the line number are in the manuscript)

> from greenwood, haply fallow deer,
> or fowl that swims the shallow mere
> you crave, then I will bring it thee,
> though I should search oer land and lea.
> No gold nor silk nor jewel bright   225
> can match my gladness and delight,
> the boy and maiden lily-fair
> that here do lie and thou didst bear'.

and ends with lines 245–252.

> His lance of ash the lord then caught,
> the wine was to his stirrup brought;
> his black horse bore him oer the land
> to the green boughs of Broceliand,
> to the green glades where the listening deer
> seldom hunter or hoof do hear;
> his horn they harken, as they stare and stand,
> echoing in Broceliand.

The following complete page of 46 lines, page 5 of those clipped together, opens with 'Though spring and summer wear and fade' and depicts the passing of seasons and with the return of spring the birth of twin children as in the *Welsh Review* version. Written in the left margin and marked for insertion are the eight lines of dialogue spoken by the anonymous 'humbler men' who comment on the lord's good fortune that, 'Would every prayer were answered twice!' and end with 'long live her lord her joy to share!' The page ends with the Lord's speech, 'If, more than gold or jewel rare.' It is in this draft that the terms *Aotrou* and *Itroun* appear for the first time, used in direct address between the Lord and Lady. The manuscript is untitled, but the word <u>Aotrou</u> (underlined) is written in the margin beside the first lines of the last page.

There is as well a complete fair manuscript copy of 12 pages with a separate hand-written title-page: 'Aotrou & Itroun', the sub-title '<u>Lord and Lady</u>' and below in parenthesis '(a Breton Lay)'. The pages are numbered consecutively, and the last page bears the notation in Tolkien's hand 'JRRT Sept. 23 1930' (see Christopher's Note on the Text, p. xi).

The *lai* was a popular poetic form in twelfth- and thirteenth-century France. The best and best-known *lais* are by a twelfth-century poet known only by the name she gave herself, Marie de France, regarded by many as the greatest woman poet of the Middle Ages. Marie's *lais*, she tells us, are retellings in French of tales 'from which the Bretons made their *lais*', (Hanning and Ferrante 30), although there are no earlier Breton *lais* by which we can corroborate her statement. Editions of Marie's *Lais* were among the books in Tolkien's library, and it is not inconceivable that in recasting 'The Corrigan' II as a *lai* Tolkien was consciously following Marie's example.

In form the *lai* is a long narrative in rhymed, octosyllabic couplets, traditionally focused on a magical or supernatural object – in this case the magic potion of the fay. A legitimate comparison can be made with Tolkien's *Lay of Leithian* with its focus on the Silmaril. Although it has no French antecedent, it is in form and subject matter a traditional *lai*. It is worth recalling, here, that Christopher Tolkien dates the writing to the period (1930) when Tolkien was also working on *The Lay of Leithian*.

AOTROU & ITROUN

(Fair copy manuscript)

**
*

In Britain's land beyond the seas
the wind blows ever through the trees;
in Britain's land beyond the waves
are stony shores and stony caves.

There stands a ruined toft now green,   5
where lords and ladies once were seen;
where towers were piled above the trees,
and watchmen scanned the sailing seas.

　Of old a lord in archéd hall
with standing stones yet grey and tall   10
there dwelt, till dark his doom befell,
as yet the Briton harpers tell.
No children he had his house to cheer,
his gardens lacked their laughter clear;
though wife he wooed and wed with ring,   15
who long her love to bed did bring,
his bowers were empty, vain his hoard,
without an heir did[26] to land and sword.

* * *

---

[26] See Commentary p. 84.

. Aotrou & Itroun .

In Britain's land beyond the seas
the wind blows ever through the trees;
in Britain's land beyond the waves
are stony shores and stony caves.

There stands a ruined toft now green,
where lords and ladies once were seen;
where towers were piled above the trees,
and watchmen scanned the sailing seas.

Of old a lord in archéd hall
with standing stones yet grey and tall
there dwelt, till dark his doom befell,
as yet the Briton harpers tell.
No children he had his house to cheer,
his gardens lacked their laughter clear;
though wife he wooed and wed with ring,
who long her love to bed did bring,
his bowers were empty, vain his hoard,
without an heir did to land and sword.
His hungry heart did lonely eld,
his house's end, his banners felled,
his tomb unheeded, long forbode,
till brooding black his mind did goad
a mad and monstrous rede to take,
pondering oft at night awake.

A witch there was, who webs did weave
to snare the heart and wits to reave,
who span dark spells with spider-craft,
and, spinning, soundless shook and laughed;
and draughts she brewed of strength and dread
to bind the live and stir the dead.
In a cave she housed, where winging bats
their harbour sought, and owls and cats
from hunting came with mournful cries
night-stalking near with needle-eyes.
In the homeless hills was that hollow dale,
black was its bowl, its brink was pale;
there silent sat she on seat of stone
at cavern's mouth in the hills alone;
there silent waited. Few there came,
or man, or beast that man doth tame.

His hungry heart did lonely eld,
his house's end, his banners felled,   20
his tomb unheeded, long forbode,
till brooding black his mind did goad
a mad and monstrous rede[27] to take,
pondering oft at night awake.

A witch there was, who webs did weave   25
to snare the heart and wits to reave,
who span dark spells with spider-craft,
and, spinning, soundless shook and laughed;
and draughts she brews of strength and dread
to bind the live and stir the dead.   30
In a cave she housed, where winging bats
their harbour sought, and owls and cats
from hunting came with mournful cries
night-stalking near with needle-eyes.
In the homeless hills was that hollow dale,   35
black was its bowl, its brink was pale;
there silent sat she on a seat of stone
at cavern's mouth in the hills alone;
there silent waited. Few there came,
or man, or beast that man doth tame.   40

Thither one day, as drooping red
the sullen sun was sinking dead,
and darkly from the mountain-rims
the slanting shadows reached their limbs,

---

[27] decision, resolve, plan

that lord, alone, with lagging feet   45
came halting to her stony seat,
as if his quest he now half rued,
half loathed his purpose yet pursued.

   In Britain's land beyond the waves
are stony hills and stony caves;   50
the wind blows ever over hills
and hollow caves with wailing fills.

   His words came faltering on the wind,
while silent sat the crone and grinned;
but words he needed few – her eyes   55
were dark and piercing; filled with lies,
yet needle-keen all lies to probe.
He shuddered neath his sable robe.
His name she knew, his need, his thought,
the hunger that thither him had brought;   60
and ere his halting words were spent,
she rose and nodded, head she bent,
and stooped into her darkening cave,
whose mouth was gaping like a grave.
Returning swift in hand she laid   65
a phial of glass so fairly made
'twas wonder in that houseless place
to see its cold and gleaming grace;
and therewithin a liquid lay
as pale as water thin and grey   70
that no light sees and no air moves
lifeless lying under rocky rooves.

He thanked her trembling, proffering gold
to clawlike fingers shrunk and old.
The thanks she took not, nor the fee,   75
but laughing croaked: 'Nay, we shall see!
Let thanks abide, till thanks be earned!
Men say such potions some have burned,
and some have cheated, unavailing,
working naught. I'll have no railing.   80
My fee shall wait, till fee I earn,
and, maybe, master, you return,
to pay me richly, or with gold,
or with what other wealth you hold.'

In Brittany the ways are long,   85
and woods are dark with danger strong;
the sound of seas is in the leaves
and wonder walks the forest-eaves.

The way was long, the woods were dark;
at last the lord beheld the spark   90
of living light from window high,
and knew his halls and towers nigh.
At last he slept in weary sleep
beside his wife, in dreaming deep,
and wandered with his children dear   95
in gardens fair, yet girt with fear,
while dim the fingers slow did crawl
of creeping dawn across the wall.

The morning came with weathers fair,
for windy rain had washed the air,   100
and blue and cloudless, clean and high,
above the hills was arched the sky,
and foaming in the northern breeze
beneath the sky there shone the seas.
Arising then to greet the sun,   105
and day with a new thought begun,
that lord in guise of joy him clad,
and masked his mind in seeming glad;
his mouth unwonted laughter used,
and words of mirth. He oft had mused,   110
walking alone with furrowed brow;
a feast he bade prepare him now.
And 'Itroun mine' he said, 'my life,
'tis long that thou hast been my wife.
Too swiftly by in love do slip   115
our gentle years, and as a ship
returns to port, we soon shall find
again that morn of spring we mind,
when we were wed, and bells were rung;
but still we love, and still are young.   120
A merry feast we'll make this year,
and there shall sit nor sigh nor tear;
and we will feign our love begun
in joy anew, anew to run
down happy paths – and yet, maybe,   125
we'll pray that this time we may see
our hearts' desire more quick draw nigh
than yet we have seen it, thou and I;
for virtue is in hope and prayer':
so spake he gravely, seeming-fair.   130

In Britain's land across the seas
the spring is merry in the trees;
in Britain's land the birds do pair,
when leaves are long and flowers are fair.

A merry feast that year they made   135
when blossom white on bush was laid;
there minstrels sang, and wine was poured,
and flowers were hung on wall and board.
A silver cup that lord there raised,
and smiling on the lady gazed: 140
'I drink to thee for health and bliss,
fair love,' he said, 'and with this kiss
the pledge I pass. Come, drink it deep!
The wine is sweet, the cup is steep!'

The wine was red, the cup was grey;   145
but blended there a liquid lay
as pale as water thin and frore
in hollow pools of caverns hoar.

She drank it, laughing with her eyes:
'Aotrou, lord and love!' she cries,   150
'all hail! and life both long and sweet –
wherein desire at last to meet!'

Dear love had been between the twain;
but stronger now it grew again,
and days ran on in great delight,   155
with hope at morn and mirth at night;
and in the garden of his dream
the fence of fear but faint did seem,

a far-off shadow at the edge
of lawns of sunlight without hedge: 160
there children two, a boy and maid,
yet half-imagined, danced and played.

   Though spring and summer wear and fade,
though flowers fall, and leaves are laid,
and winter winds his trumpets loud   165
mid snows that fell and forest shroud;
though roaring seas upon the shore
go long and white, and neath the door
the wind cries with houseless voice,
yet fire and song may men rejoice,   170
till as a ship returns to port
the spring comes back to field and court.

   A song there falls from windows high,
like gold that droppeth from the sky
soft in the early eve of spring.   175
'Why do they play? Why do they sing?'

'Light may she lie, our lady fair!
Too long hath been her cradle bare.
Yestreve there came as I passed by
the cry of babes from windows high –   180
twin children, I am told, there be.
Light may they lie and sleep, all three!'

'Would every prayer were answered twice!
Half or nothing must oft suffice
for humbler men, though they wear their knees   185
more bare than lords, as oft one sees.'

'Not every lord wins such fair grace.
Come, wish them speed with kinder face!
Light may she lie, my lady fair;
long live her lord her joy to share!'   190

    A manchild and an infant maid
as lilies fair were in cradle laid,
and mirth was in their mother's heart
like music slow in deeps apart.
Glad was that lord, as grave he stood   195
beside her bed of carven wood.
'Now full,' he said, 'is granted me
both hope and prayer, and what of thee?
Is 't not, fair love, most passing sweet
the heart's desire at last to meet?   200

'Yet if thy heart still longing hold,
or lightest wish remain untold,
that will I find and bring to thee,
though I should ride both land and sea!'

'Aotrou mine,' she said, ''tis sweet   205
at last the heart's desire to meet
thus after waiting, after prayer,
thus after hope and nigh despair.
I would not have thee ride nor run
from me beside nor from thy son!   210

– yet after sickness, after pain
oft cometh hunger sharp again.'

'Nay, Itroun, if thirst or hunger strange
for bird or beast on earth that range,
for wine, or water from what well   215
in any secret fount or dell,
thee vex,' he smiled, 'now swift declare!
If, more than gold or jewel rare,
from greenwood, haply, fallow deer,
or fowl that swims the shallow mere   220
thou cravest, I will bring it thee,
though I should hunt oer land and lea.
No gold nor silk nor jewel bright
can match my gladness and delight,
the boy and maiden lily-fair   225
that here do lie and thou didst bear.'

'Aotrou, lord,' she said, ''tis true,
a longing strong and sharp I knew,
in dream, for water cool and clear
and venison of the greenwood deer;   230
for waters crystal-clear and cold
and deer no earthly forests hold;
and still in waking comes unsought
the foolish wish to vex my thought.
But I would not have thee ride nor run   235
from me beside nor from thy son!'

In Brittany beyond the seas
the wind blows ever through the trees;
in Brittany the forest pale
marches slow oer hill and dale.   240
There seldom ever horns were wound,
and seldom ran there horse or hound.

His lance of ash the lord then caught,
the wine was to his stirrup brought.
His black horse bore him oer the land   245
to the green boughs of Broceliande,
to the green dales where the listening deer
seldom hunter or hoof do hear –
his horn they hearken, as they stare and stand,
echoing in Broceliande.   250

Beneath the deepest woodland's eaves
a white doe startled under leaves;
strangely she glistered in the sun
as leaping forth she turned to run.
He hunted her from forest-eaves   255
into the twilight under leaves.
Ever he rode on reckless after,
and heard no sound of distant laughter.
The earth was shaken under hoof,
till the boughs were bent into a roof,   260
and the sun was woven in a snare;
and still there was laughter on the air.

The sun was fallen. Dim there fell
a silence in the forest dell.
No sight nor slot of doe was seen,   265
but shadows dark the trees between;
and then a longing sharp and strange
for deer that free and fair do range
him vexed, for venison of the beast
whereon no mortal hunt shall feast;   270
for water crystal-clear and cold
that never in holy fountain rolled.

The sun was lost; all green was grey;
but twinkled the fountain of the fay
before her cavern on silver sand   275
under dark boughs of Broceliande.
Soft was the grass and clear the pool;
he laved his face in water cool,
and then he saw her on silver chair
before her cavern. Pale her hair,   280
slow was her smile, and white her hand
beckoning in Broceliande.

The moon through leaves then clear and cold
her long hair lit; through comb of gold
she drew her locks, and down they fell   285
as the fountain falling in the dell.
He heard her voice and it was cold
as echo from the world of old,
ere fire was found or iron hewn,
when young was mountain under moon.   290
He heard her voice like water falling
or wind along a long shore calling,
yet sweet the words: 'We meet again
here after waiting, after pain!
Aotrou! lo, thou hast returned –   295
perchance some kindness I have earned?
What hast thou, lord, to give to me
whom thou hast come thus far to see?'

'I know thee not, I know thee not,
nor ever saw thy darkling grot.   300
O corrigan, 'twas not for thee
I hither came a-hunting free!'

'How darest then, my water wan
to trouble thus, or look me on?
For this at least I claim my fee,   305
if ever thou wouldst wander free.
With love thou shalt me here requite,
for here is long and sweet the night;
in druery dear thou here shalt deal,
in bliss more deep than mortals feel.'   310

'I give no love. My love is wed;
my wife now lieth in child-bed,
and I curse the beast that cheated me
and drew me to this dell to thee.'

Her smiling ceased and slow she said: 315
'Forget thy wife; for thou shalt wed
anew with me, or stand as stone
and wither lifeless and alone,
as stone beside the fountain stand
forgotten in Broceliande.'   320

'I will not stand here turned to stone;
but I will leave thee cold, alone,
and I will ride to mine own home
and the waters blest of Christendom.'

'But three days then and thou shalt die;   325
in three days on thy bier lie!'

'In three days I shall live at ease,
and die but when it God doth please
in eld, or in some time to come
in the brave wars of Christendom!'   330

   In Britain's land beyond the waves
are forest dim and secret caves;
in Britain's land the wind doth bear
the sound of bells along the air
that mingles with the sound of seas   335
for ever moving in the trees.

   The way was long and woven wild;
the hunter, who to wife and child
did haste, at last he heard a bell
in some spire ring the sacring knell;   340
at last he saw the tilth of men,
escaped from thicket and from fen;
the hoar and houseless hills he passed
and weary at his gates him cast.

'Good steward! if thou love me well,   345
bid make my bed! My heart doth swell;
my limbs are numb with heavy sleep,
as there did drowsy poison creep.
All night, as in a fevered maze,
I have ridden dark and winding ways.'   350

   To bed they brought him and to sleep,
fitful, uneasy; there did creep
the shreds of dreams, wherein no more
was sun nor garden, but the roar

of angry sea and angry wind;   355
and there a dark fate leered and grinned,
or changed – and where a fountain fell
a corrigan was singing in a dell;
a white hand as the fountain spilled
a phial of glass with water filled.   360

He woke at eve, and murmured: 'ringing
of bells within my ears, and singing,
a singing is beneath the moon.
I fear my death is meted soon.
Grieve her not yet, nor yet do tell,   365
though I am wounded with a spell!
But two days more, and then I die!
And I would have had her sweetly lie,
and sweet arise; and live yet long,
and see our children hale and strong.'   370

His words they little understood,
but cursed the fevers of the wood,
and to their lady no word spoke.
Ere second morn was old, she woke,
and to her women standing near   375
gave greeting with a merry cheer:
'Good people, lo! the morn is bright!
Say, did my lord return ere night,
and tarries now with hunting worn?'

'Nay, lady, he came not with the morn;   380
but ere men candles set on board,
thou wilt have tidings of thy lord;
or hear his feet to thee returning,
ere candles in the eve are burning.'

Ere the third morn was wide she woke,   385
and eager greeted them, and spoke:
'Behold the morn is cold and grey,
and why is my lord so long away?
I do not hear his feet returning
neither at evening nor at morning.'   390
'We do not know, we cannot say,'
they answered and they turned away.

Now many days had seen the light
her gentle babes in swaddling white;
and she arose and left her bed,   395
and called her maidens and she said:
'My lord must soon return. Come, bring
my fairest raiments. Stone on ring
and pearl on thread, that him may please
when, coming weary back, he sees.'   400

She looked from window tall and high,
and felt a breeze go coldly by;
she saw it pass from tree to tree,
and clouds that lay from hill to sea.
She heard no horn and heard no hoof,   405
but rain came pattering on the roof;
in Brittany she heard the waves
on sounding shore in hollow caves.

The day wore on till it was old;
she heard the bells that solemn tolled.   410
'Good folk, what is this noise they make?
In tower I hear the slow bells shake.
Why sing the white priests chanting low,
as though one to the grave did go?'

'A man unhappy here there came   415
a while agone. His horse was lame;
sickness was on him, and he fell
before our gates, or so they tell.
Here he was harboured, but to-day
he died, and passeth now the way   420
we all must go, to church to lie
on bier before the altar high.'

She looked upon them, dark and deep,
and saw them in the shadows weep.
'Then tall, and fair, and brave was he,   425
or tale of sorrow there must be
concerning him, which still ye keep,
if for a stranger thus ye weep!
What know ye more? Ah say, ah say!'
They answered not, and turned away.   430

'Ah me,' she said, 'that I could sleep
this night, or least that I could weep!'
But all night long she tossed and turned,
and in her limbs a fever burned;
and yet when sudden under sun   435
a fairer morning was begun,

'Good folk, to church I wend,' she said,
'My raiment choose, or robe of red,
or robe of blue, or white and fair,
silver and gold; I do not care.'   440

'Nay, lady,' said they, 'none of these.
The custom used as now one sees
for women that to churching go
is robe of black and walking slow.'

    In robe of black and walking slow   445
the lady did to churching go,
in hand a candle small and white,
her face so fair, her hair so bright.
They passed beneath the western door;
there dark within on stony floor   450
a bier before the altar high,
and candles yellow stood thereby.
The watchful candles dim and tall
a light let on the blazon fall,
the arms and banner of her lord: 455
in vain his pride, in vain his hoard.

    To bed they brought her, swift to sleep
for ever cold, though there did weep
her women by her dark bedside,
or babes in cradle waked and cried.   460

There was singing slow at dead of night,
and many feet, and taper-light.
At morn there rang the sacring knell
and far men heard the single bell,

sad, though the sun lay on the land;   465
though far in dim Broceliande
a fountain silver flowed and fell
within a darkly-woven dell;
though in the homeless hills a dale
was filled with laughter cold and pale.   470

    Beside her lord at last she lay
in their long home beneath the clay;
and though their children lived yet long
or played in garden hale and strong,
they saw it not, nor found it sweet   475
their hearts' desire at last to meet.

    In Brittany beyond the waves
are sounding shores and hollow caves;
in Brittany beyond the seas
the wind blows ever through the trees.   480
Of lord and lady all is said:
God rest their souls, who now are dead.
Sad is the note, and sad the lay;
but mirth we meet not every day.
God keep us all in hope and prayer,   485
from evil rede and from despair,
by waters blest of Christendom
to dwell, until at last we come
to joy of Heaven where is queen
the maiden Mary pure and clean.   490

NOTES AND COMMENTARY

without an heir did to land and sword (l. 18). The 'did' in this line is almost certainly mis-copied from the following line 19, 'His hungry heart did lonely eld.' The added word ruins the scansion, the grammar and the meaning of line 18. Nevertheless, it went uncorrected by the poet, and is therefore here retained.

a mad and monstrous rede (l. 23). Carried over from line 12 of the fragment. Compare with 'cold counsel' in the parallel passage in the published poem. Tolkien's use of 'rede' here is typical of his tendency to go out of his way to use an archaic form for a conventional meaning. The usual definition of *rede*, from Old English *ræd* from Old Norse *ráð*, is 'counsel, advice', not as here, 'decision' or 'resolve'. The editorial 'mad and monstrous' makes a judgment of the lord which is lacking in the published poem.

THE TYPESCRIPT

One more iteration of the poem occurs before the final version published in *The Welsh Review*. This is a typescript with extensive emendations, additions and transpositions added in ink in Tolkien's hand. It is the typescript version, as Christopher Tolkien points out, which became the basis and probable copy-text for the final version.

The typescript begins with a title-page, tattered and dog-eared along the upper edge, with the words 'Aotrou & Itroun' hand-lettered in ink. Below them is the subtitle in typewriter italic 'Lord and Lady' and further down the page and again typewritten, A 'Breton Lay'. Below that in Tolkien's hand is written: 'by J.R.R. Tolkien'. At the bottom of the page, upside down and with the letters reversed, are the typewritten words, 'night-stalking near with needle-eyes', and below that, 'in the homeless hills was that hollow dale, black was'. The line runs off the page.

The typescript itself comprises fourteen pages; the length of the poem, without the marginal additions and emendations, is 490 lines, the same number as the manuscript fair copy on which it is based. The final *Welsh Review* version (reproduced above) has 506 lines. Tolkien's revisions to the typescript, adding in some places, removing in others, extended the poem by 16 lines.

⊹ Aotrou & Itroun ⊹

In Britain's land beyond the seas
the wind blows ever through the trees;
in Britain's land beyond the waves
are stony shores and stony caves.

There stands a ruined toft now green
where lords and ladies once were seen,
where towers were piled above the trees
and watchmen scanned the sailing seas.
Of old a lord in archéd hall
with standing stones yet grey and tall
there dwelt, till dark his doom befell,
as still the Briton harpers tell.

No children he had his house to cheer,
nor filled his courts with ~~old vassans lacked their~~ laughter clear;
though wife he wooed and wed with ring,
who love to board and bed did bring,
his pride was empty, vain his hoard,
without an heir to land and sword.

~~his pulses beat did lonely oft,~~
~~his house's end, his honour's ruin,~~
~~his race unended, long forbode,~~
~~till broodings black his mind did~~
~~a sad and monstrous road to take,~~
~~boodings oft at night awake.~~

[left margin handwritten:]
And pondering oft at night awake
his darkened mind would
.... make
of lonely age, and death; to end
unheeded what strangers in's room
with other names and this child
were masters of his halls and fields.
This counsel cold he took at last:
his hope from light to darkness
passed.

[right margin handwritten:]
And pondering oft at night awake
His darkened mind would vision make
Of lonely age, and death; his tomb
Unkept, while strangers in his room
with other names and other shields
were masters of his halls and fields.
Thus counsel cold he took at last:
His hope from light to darkness passed.

A witch there was, who ~~wove~~ *could* weave
to snare the heart and wits to reave,
who span dark spells with spider-craft,
and *as she span she softly* ~~twisted counsels .... and~~ laughed;
A
~~she brewed~~ she brewed of strength and dream
to bind the *quick* and stir the dead.
In a cave she housed where winging bats
their harbour sought, and owls and bats
from hunting came with mournful cries,

COMMENTARY

The typescript which was the basis for *The Lay of Aotrou and Itroun* as published in *The Welsh Review* version is a window into Tolkien's creative process, showing the final steps in his journey from early 'Corrigan' to final, definitive *Aotrou and Itroun*; from ballad to *lai*; and from folktale to tragedy. There are revisions on every page. Some are mere substitutions of one word for another, but many are substantial cancellations and rewritings, in one case of nine lines. A separate slip marked for insertion contains seventeen lines, and even that has cancellations and additions. It has not been thought practical to reproduce the entire typescript, but the preceding sample page will give some idea of the extent and nature of the changes. A few examples of Tolkien's revision process will show both his editorial and creative mind at work.

Lines 19 through 24 were originally typed as follows:

> His hungry heart did lonely eld,
> his house's end, his banner felled,
> his tomb unheeded, long forebode,
> till brooding black his mind did goad
> a mad and monstrous rede to take,
> pondering oft at night awake.

These are copied word for word from the fair manuscript. But they are then crossed out, and in the left-hand margin the following lines are jotted for insertion:

> And pondering oft at night awake
> his darkened mind would visions make
> of lonely age, and death, his tomb
> unheeded while strangers in his room
> with other names and other shields
> were masters of his halls and fields.
> Thus counsel cold he took at last,
> his hope from light to darkness passed.

The changes from typescript to first revision are substantial. The revision is longer by two lines; the last line becomes the first line; the felled banner is omitted; the 'unheeded' tomb becomes 'unkept' instead, altering inattention to neglect; the lord's 'brooding black' mind becomes 'his darkened mind', suggesting a change rather than a state or condition. Of special importance is the addition of the last two lines, changing 'rede' to 'counsel' and shifting the alliteration from 'mad and monstrous' to 'cold', where it emphasizes 'counsel', and charting the passage of hope from light to darkness.

But Tolkien did not stop there. These lines also are crossed out, and in the corresponding right-hand margin he has carefully written:

> ~~And~~ Thus pondering oft at night awake
> His darkened mind would visions make
> Of lonely age and death; his tomb
> Unkept while strangers in his room

> With other names and other shields
> Were masters of his halls and fields.
> Thus counsel cold he took at last:
> His hope from light to darkness passed.

These changes are smaller, evidence of fine-tuning. The replacement of 'And' by 'Thus' substitutes an adverbial comment for a simple connective. There is a ghost 's' at the end of 'vision' in this revision, possibly added in pencil but so lightly that you have to use a magnifying glass to read it. The comma after 'counsel cold he took at last' is now a colon, making the passage of hope from light to dark the direct outcome of 'counsel cold'.

Of particular interest is the separate sheet inserted between pages 10–11 and eleven and intended to replace lines 351–360 of page ten. The passage takes place on the lord's return to his house. Here is the typescript version, circled in ink and crossed out.

> To bed they brought him and to sleep,
> fitful, uneasy; there did creep
> the shreds of dreams, wherein no more
> was sun nor garden, but the roar
> of angry sea and angry wind;
> and there a dark face leered and grinned,
> or changed – and where a fountain fell
> a corrigan was singing in a dell;
> a white hand as the fountain spilled
> a phial of glass with water filled.

Here are the lines written on the separate sheet:

To bed they brought him and to sleep:
in sunless thickets tangled deep
he dreamed, and wandering found no more
the garden green, but on the shore
the sea went moaning in the wind;
a face before him leered and grinned:
Now^{Now it is} tis earned, come bring to me
my fee it cried a voice said, bring my fee!
Beside a fountain falling cold
{? And then he saw a fountain cold
the Corrigan now greyed shrunk and old
was sitting singing; in her claw
a comb of bony teeth he saw
with which she^{broken cloven hand}raked her withered tress
    tresses hoar^{grey}
and^{but} in her other hand she bore ?] there lay
a phial of glass with water filled
that from the bitter fountain spilled.

While the many revisions address different aspects of the poem, one major change, first evidenced in the fragment, is Tolkien's addition of a motive for the lord, the careful development of the processes of his mind and their progression from foreboding to resolve and thence to action. The story thus is more *Macbeth* than *Oedipus*, not a tale of a man caught unknowingly in the toils of fate, but the tragedy of a man going willfully down the wrong road, whose fall into error makes him the architect of his own destiny.

A second change concerns the development of the *corrigan*. She has three scenes in the finished poem, as contrasted with two in the fair manuscript copy, one in 'The Corrigan' II, and none at all in 'The Corrigan' I. Moreover, one of the three scenes plays out as the dream of the sleeping lord, shifting the focus from the supernatural to the psychological. Here the lord sees in his sleep the *corrigan* not as the 'beautiful fay' of the epigraph and her other appearances as the seductive fairy of the fountain, but in her alternate shape of a withered hag.

The direction of these revisions, and indeed of the general changes from poem to poem, take the story into ever deeper and darker territory. Rather than beginning with the birth of twin children, as does the original Breton poem and Tolkien's shorter 'Lay', his later version makes the lord's childlessness the engine of his doom, his 'mad and monstrous' resolve to seek the fay a symptom of his darkening mind, and juxtaposes the physical allure of the fay against her 'withered' and 'bony' image in the lord's dream. No work of Tolkien's says more about his concept of the dark side of faërie, his belief in the very real peril of the perilous realm, and his awareness of its pitfalls for the unwary and its dungeons for the overbold.

PART FOUR

COMPARATIVE VERSES

COMPARATIVE VERSES

On several occasions in his essays and letters Tolkien asserted his deep conviction that language and myth are inseparable one from the other; each being the outgrowth of the other; each dependent on the other for its essential meaning. The paired notions that a world created by the language that describes it generates the language of the world it describes led him directly from his study of real-world myths in their proper languages (including Anglo-Saxon, Old Norse, Finnish and Breton) to his invented world and the languages he developed for its peoples' expression.

Comparison of the verses offered below from the Breton original, Villemarqué's French paraphrase, two contemporary English translations by Thomas Keightley and Tom Taylor, and Tolkien's version of *The Lay of Aotrou and Itroun* will illustrate the principle. Even without a familiarity with any of the languages shown, it is possible to recognize on the page and feel in the mouth differences in shape and sound and delivery among the original Breton as given by Villemarqué, and the French and two competing English translations, and to compare those with Tolkien's renderings of the same poems.

To reproduce all the poems in all the languages is beyond the scope of this volume, and, even if practical, would be a demanding chore for even the most diligent readers. But it is to be hoped that the representative sampling here given, aided by some knowledge of the plots and characters of the story involved, will offer a taste, at least, of Tolkien's dictum that 'mythology is language and language is mythology' (*TOFS* 181).

The verses are presented without commentary in the expectation that they will speak for themselves.

Opening Verses: Breton, French, English

Villemarqué's Breton
'Aotrou Nann Hag ar Gorrigan', 1846

Ann aotrou Nann hag he briet
Iaouankik-flamm oent dimezet,
Iaouankik-flamm dispartiet.

Villemarqué's French
'Le Seigneur Nann et la Fée', 1846

Le siegneur Nann et son épose
ont été fiancés bien jeunes,
bien jeunes désunis.

Tom Taylor's English
'The Lord Nann and the Fairy', 1865

The good Lord Nann and his fair bride,
Were young when wedlock's knot was tied –
Were young when death did them divide.

Thomas Keightley's English
'Lord Nann and the Korrigan', 1882

The Lord Nann and his bride so fair
In early youth united were,
In early youth divided were.

Opening Verses: J.R.R. Tolkien Poems

'The Corrigan' II, 1930

See how high in their joy they ride
The young earl and his young bride!
May nought ever their joy divide,
    Though the world be full of wonder.

The Lay of Aotrou and Itroun
(*The Welsh Review*, 1945)

In Britain's land beyond the seas
the wind blows ever through the trees;
in Britain's land beyond the waves
are stony shores and stony caves.

There stands a ruined toft now green
where lords and ladies once were seen,
where towers were piled above the trees
and watchmen scanned the sailing seas.
Of old a lord in archéd hall
with standing stones yet grey and tall
there dwelt, till dark his doom befell,
as still the Briton harpers tell.

No child he had his house to cheer,
to fill his with laughter clear;
though wife he wooed and wed with ring,
who love to board and bed did bring,
his pride was empty, vain his hoard,
without an heir to land and sword.

Closing Verses: Breton, French, English

Villemarqué's Breton
'Aotrou Nann Hag ar Gorrigan'

Gwelet diou wezen derv sevel
Diouc'h ho bez nevez d'ann uc'hel;

Ha war ho brank diou c'houlmik wenn,
Hag hi ken dreo hakel laouen,

Eno 'kana da c'houlou de,
Hag o nijal d'ann env goude.

Villemarqué's French
'Le Seigneur Nann et la Feé'

De voir deux chênes s'elever de leur tombe nouvelle dans les airs;
Et sur leurs branchés, deux colombes blanches, sautillantes et gaies,
Qui chantèrant au lever de l'aurore, et prirent ensuite leur volée
vers les cieux.

Tom Taylor's English
'The Lord Nann and the Fairy'

Next morn from the grave to oak-trees fair,
shot lusty boughs high up in air;

And in their boughs – oh wondrous sight! –
Two happy doves, all snowy white –

That sang as ever the morn did rise;
And then flew up – into the skies!

Thomas Keightley's English
'Lord Nann and the Korrigan'

To see two oak-trees themselves rear
From the new-made grave into the air;

And on their branches two doves white,
Who there were hopping gay and light;

Which sang when rose the morning ray
And then toward heaven sped away.

Closing Verses: J.R.R. Tolkien Poems

'The Corrigan' II, 1930

They laid her beside him in the night.
I heard bells ring. There was taperlight.
    Priests were chanting a litany.
Darkness lay upon the land,
But afar in pale Broceliand
    There sang a fay in Brittany.

The Lay of Aotrou and Itroun
(*The Welsh Review*, 1945)

            the sun lay on the land;
while deep in dim Broceliande
a silver fountain flowed and fell
within a darkly woven dell,
and in the homeless hills a dale
was filled with laughter cold and pale.

Beside her lord at last she lay
in their long home beneath the clay;
and if their children lived yet long,
or played in garden hale and strong,

they saw it not, nor found it sweet
their heart's desire at last to meet.

In Brittany beyond the waves
are sounding shores and hollow caves;
in Brittany beyond the seas
the wind blows ever through the trees.

Of lord and lady all is said:
God rest their souls, who now are dead!
Sad is the note and sad the lay,
but mirth we meet not every day.
God keep us all in hope and prayer
from evil rede and from despair,
by waters blest of Christendom
to dwell, until at last we come
to joy of Heaven where is queen
the maiden Mary pure and clean.

WORKS CITED

Briggs, Katherine. *The Vanishing People*. New York: Pantheon Books, 1978.

Denham, Michael Aislabie. *The Denham Tracts*, Reprinted from the original, ed. Dr. James Hardy. 2 vols. London: David Nutt for the Folklore Society, 1892–95.

Evans-Wentz, Walter. *The Fairy-Faith in Celtic Countries*. University Books, Inc., 1966.

Houghton, John William and Janet Brennan Croft, Nancy Martsch, John D. Rateliff and Robin Anne Reid. *Tolkien in the New Century: Essays in Honor of Tom Shippey*. Jefferson, NC: McFarland & Company, Inc., 2014.

Keightley, Thomas. *The Fairy Mythology*. London: George Bell & Sons, 1882.

Kirk, Robert. *The Secret Commonwealth of Elves, Fauns and Fairies*. Stirling: [The Observer Press] Eneas MacKay, 1933.

MacKillop, James. *Dictionary of Celtic Mythology*. Oxford University Press, 1998.

Marie de France. *The Lais of Marie de France*, trans. Robert Hanning & Joan Ferrante. New York: E.P. Dutton, 1978.

Scull, Christina and Wayne Hammond. *The J.R.R. Tolkien Companion and Guide*, Vol. 1, *Chronology*. Boston: Houghton Mifflin Company, 2006.

Shippey, Tom. *The Road to Middle-earth*, Revised and Expanded Edition. London: HarperCollins*Publishers*, 2005.

Taylor, Tom. *Ballads and Songs of Brittany*, Translated From The 'Barzaz-Breiz' of Vicomte Hersart de la Villemarqué. London: MacMillan and Co., 1865.

Tolkien, J.R.R. *The Lord of the Rings*, 2nd Edition. 3 vols. Boston: Houghton Mifflin Company, 1967.

——. *The Letters of J.R.R. Tolkien*, ed. Humphrey Carpenter. Boston: Houghton Mifflin Company, 1981.

——. *Tolkien on Fairy-Stories*, Expanded edition, ed. Verlyn Flieger & Douglas A. Anderson. London: HarperCollins*Publishers*, 2008.

——. *The Lays of Beleriand*, ed. Christopher Tolkien. Boston: Houghton Mifflin Company, 1985.

——. *The Monsters and the Critics,* ed. Christopher Tolkien. London: George Allen & Unwin, 1983.

——. *Sauron Defeated*, ed. Christopher Tolkien. London: Harper-Collins*Publishers*, 1992.

Villemarqué, Théodore Hersart de la. *Barzaz-Breiz: Chants Populaire de la Bretagne*. Tome Premier. Paris: A. Franck, 1846.

Yates, Jessica. 'The Source of "The Lay of Aotrou and Itroun"', in *Leaves From the Tree*. London: The Tolkien Society, 1991 (pp. 63–71).